Text copyright © 2015 Steve A. Reed
All Rights Reserved

Chapter One

Clae is the place where things never happen. The daily melodramatics that populate our time are just the everyday drama of existence in Clae. The polyphonic sounds of technology surround us from the trill of mobile phones to the roar of passenger aircraft, the omnipresent rumble of traffic and the banshee howl of emergency vehicles: Clae knows only the white noise of its own heartbeat, in the rush of the River Henry and the turning of the mill. The counterpoint being the unhurried murmur of conversation, human interaction at its most... well, Human!
If places were in reality, animate, as they often are in metaphor, then the Cities of Britain jiggle in the throes of a fit while Clae rests with its feet up, breathing steadily and nodding off from time to time.

The folklore of Clae told of three big wars, which had ravaged the country. The First World War had touched Clae because they had, at that time, been infrequently in contact with the world at large, and several of the young men had sacrificed themselves to that distant cause. The Second World War had slapped indiscriminately at many countries and scored a direct hit on the Clae Church. There had also been a third strike at the security of Clae and ironically the one that secured its boundaries.

The Ministry of Defence, in its enthusiasm for blowing up parts of the countryside, had designated the area around Clae, as a target range. For ten happy years, the boys in green had rocked the foundations of every building in Clae with various projectiles aimed at the surrounding hills.

Why they never ventured over the hills, or even targeted the place, are mysteries of the defence industry, as mystifying as why they later abandoned the site and left it quiet and fenced with signs warning about the dangers lurking within. Those dangers, be they real or imagined, kept some away. The fact that the area belonged to the Military kept others away.

The main result of the tactical withdrawal was this; the inhabitants of Clae assumed the conflict to be over, and settled back into their peaceful existence, untroubled by the Cuban missile crisis, or Chernobyl, the wars in the Gulf or the terrorists that make fear a part of life on every continent.

The lush garden - the stagnant gene pool - the lost village of Clae: nestled among the hills, forgotten by a Britain that embraces the new and technological with such fidelity, that it forgets that places like Clae ever existed.

No road goes there to pump the stale subsistence of rural commerce into an arterial one way system: the type of arrangement that encircles many towns that were once merely villages in the so-called Stockbroker belt. Roads were their ruin, but Clae has no road. In fact the only link that Clae had ever had with the world outside, had been a footpath across the rocky hills which isolate and protect, even form the boundaries of the district. If this footpath exists at all, it does so theoretically on an old ordinance survey map. The people inhabiting the closest village deemed it prudent to let that particular thoroughfare heal up; the process was actually abetted with a little judicious over ploughing.

Forgetting, forgotten, happy in its ignorance of decimal currency and satellite T.V., the populace continues on its ancient course. Resplendent in its primal superstitions and archaic practices, the village life continues unfettered by the demons of morality and law; not, as you might think, dissolved into anarchy, but worn to non- existence by the carborundum of complacent apathy.

Clae has its own small river which provides water, for a village not yet connected to the national.....anything. Even telephones failed to traverse the surrounding hills. The River

Henry, however, cunningly burrows under them to irrigate the place, keep the mill turning, and most importantly, provide water for the distillery that stands at the centre of Clae, producing the substance that caused those neighbours to purposely mislay the only path as an act of self preservation.

As the River Thames becomes the Isis as it flows through Oxford, so the River Henry is called by another name before it travels through Clae, and yet another when it emerges from the hills at some distant point having travelled underground to leave Clae. These other names may once have been known to the villagers but the regally named River Henry as it is known in Clae, is how this narrative shall respectfully dub that aqueous funiculus.

The self appointed Emperor, Lord of Clae, and protector of the West Paddock was, for many years, Fulmin Pinnock XII. With his demise at the hands of his most fickle mistress, the thrice distilled Mustard brandy, the enigmatic title rested with him in the churchyard next to the public toilets in the village square. These public facilities, built as they were, on the site, and with the rubbled remains, of Clae Church, stand as a memorial to its Norman predecessor and its entire congregation having departed together one Sunday morning in the nineteen forties, due to a wayward doodlebug. The religious element thus extracted, was a cue for the so-called 'old ways' to sidle back into the village in the person of Mathias Woodbine, visionary and erstwhile hermit. On his return to Clae (which he euphemistically referred to as civilisation) he swore abstinence from the aforementioned mustard spirit, his first true love, in favour of the spiritual needs of the locals. Thus cuckolded, his former love wrought terrible revenge upon him, plaguing him with apocalyptic visions and a prophetic gift growing increasingly obscure until the call of the hermit took him back to the hills, just in time to save him from the homicidal confusion of his flock, understandably upset by his, ever more abstract, sermons and services. This fortunate escape caused those who could manipulate such concepts, to consider the possibility that Mathias Woodbine did indeed have the gift of second sight. In fact he did, but in his case the second sight was blurred, superimposed on his first sight only marginally to the left, this due entirely to the three distillations of that most capricious liquor.

Opposite the churchyard and public convenience, stands an ornate but unimposing, brick, Victorian warehouse now the distillery where the villagers brew and distil 'MUSTIK', discovered by Boris Dyer between the wars and as responsible for the isolation of Clae as the rocky hills surrounding it. An interesting point is that since the distillery began work in the nineteen twenties, overpopulation has been of no immediate concern, as a strange and unexpected impotence affected a percentage of the populace, and continues to this day. None but Boris Dyer ever noticed that those blighted were the same ones who were the most ardent lovers of Mustik.

It must be said that Mustik is the lifeblood of this hamlet, and since a doodlebug challenged the might of the local temperance society, and won without question, some have weaned their babes on a dilution of the stuff. This situation has an element of inevitability about it since the supplies of such traditional beverages as tea and coffee disappeared along with the only footpath. Thus Mustik became, so to speak, 'the only game in town'.

    Due respect is always awarded those individuals who daily gather at the Dyer distillery, devoting themselves to the complicated manufacture of Mustik, under the guiding hand of Uther Smith, a man with a paternal eye always directed at the community, and a lazy eye always directed at the bridge of his nose. The respect he received from the villagers was due, in no small part, to his remarkable benevolence and facility for clarity of thought, the latter skill a result of his congenital inability to consume even the smallest amount of the clear substance he produced.

In the village square, two roads cross, both incomplete, which is to say that the cobblestones surfacing the crossroads dissolve into dirt track within fifteen yards of the square in all directions. Once long ago, both thoroughfares had borne long polysyllabic titles in keeping with the intended grandeur of the completed project, but only the names and the sign that bore them was ever finished. Due to the aforementioned bomb and in particular its interaction with the church, which resulted in a spectacular outward shower of masonry, even the grand sign was violently abbreviated. This, coupled with the council of elders and their custom of consuming a cup or two of Mustik at meetings and their consequent inability to recall long names (or even short ones for that matter) resulted in the adoption of the few letters still readable on the remnants of the sign passing in to common usage exactly as they appear; 'Ur' and 'Bet', incomplete names for incomplete roads, the last bastion of poetic reality.

The eastern stretch of Ur Street terminates at the door of Clae manor house once the home of Emperor Fulmin Pinnock XII, and now served as a town hall, civic centre, and most of all a library. The ancestors of Fulmin Pinnock collected the literary obscurities that populate the shelves of the 'reading room' when

Clae

Clae and the world outside it were still acquainted. Nowadays this well of knowledge is entrusted, primarily because nobody else showed the least interest, to the loving care of Ballentine Trimble, librarian. Trimble was born for the job, and reads and catalogues, rereads and files, and over the decades even finds time to grow imperceptibly older. He always speaks in a reverential whisper, 'because the books hate noise' and have a tendency to tell him so on the occasions he sits up late with a volume on the subject of central Asian weather patterns, or such like, and a mug or two of Mustik.

If the paternal affection of Uther Smith can be described as guidance, then the leadership must without question, if you know what's good for you, belong to Desdemona Pippin, midwife, seamstress, all round good egg and matriarch of Clae. Despite her apparent ferocity and imposing stature, she loved every individual in the village, and toiled tirelessly for the communal good at all times. Even Uther Smith, when he publicly denounced the mustard harvest as 'unremarkable this year' and wounded the fragile pride of Collitt Semper, chief mustard grower, even he was forced to make public an unreserved apology when the alternative was the wrath of Desdemona Pippin, thus proving that nobody is out of reach of the long judicious arm of the Matriarch.

Clae

Local trade is exactly that, the time honoured system of barter and exchange. Although pre-decimal currency does still circulate, it does not have a 'face' value, so its only remaining power in the market is in its rarity and curiosity value. The most interesting thing about the coinage is the speculation about the King depicted on them and how much older he must now be.

The work of chancellor, or the one person with a philanthropic concern about the distribution of property, is Miss Desdemona Pippin. If she can discern a need, she has the power to intervene and even ride roughshod over the usual methods of transaction, and in this capacity she describes her role as; "Doin' what's best for them what needs it"

The social structure of Clae is finely balanced and as such has to ignore such decadence as capitalism. Distributed with care, there are sufficient foodstuffs and raw material to furnish the village with the essentials of life, augmented by the skills passed on to apprentices (descendants being relatively scarce). Farming is the real basis for continued existence, but this is precarious. Disease or drought would topple this microcosm inside a year. However, providence smiles, diseases hunt other prey, the river Henry flows strongly from the rocky hills, and life goes on.

Between the wars, the demise of the last radio set had

caused such confusion that a whole day had been mislaid, with the result that when the rest of Britain bursts forth with the customary Monday morning, post-weekend mayhem, the residents of Clae are busy with their Sunday market in the village square.

On the wall of the impressive but unimposing Dyer's distillery is a clock, an old, unreliable, much loved clock, which has no concern for such absurdities as British summertime, daylight saving hours and the like. Frosty mornings, on the other hand, were something the old clock could not ignore since it required the distillery engineer Ben Calliban to place a well aimed kick at just the right point of the works to send the flywheel spinning, and time moving again, especially on a market day when nobody would trade until the clock stood at ten.

Some will have spotted, by now, a distinct break from tradition regarding names. Here in Clae a child's name is chosen from the dusty collection of old books at the library. With Shakespeare being a strong favourite, the names chosen for their tonal qualities rather than associations, can make for some unusual choices, particularly when surnames are no longer inherited but chosen by the parents, hence Fulmin Pinnock XII was from a long line of nobody named Pinnock, the suffix, XII, being part of the name rather than an indicator of antecedents numbered eleven, ten, nine, and so on and so forth, third, second etcetera.

One crisp Monday morning when, according to the wildly inaccurate distillery clock, the hour in Clae was ten; the Sunday market began to coagulate in the village square. Collitt Semper, the top mustard grower in Clae, spotted a weary looking woman of late middle age, visibly sagging with the effort of placing one trembling foot before another. Collitt, being a caring soul, rushed to her side and pulled up a nearby palette for the weary woman to sit upon.

Now, the early morning arrival of tired people is not uncommon in Clae because the name of Boris Dyer lives on in the shape of countless ugly hangovers, but the arrival of this woman was worthy of note, not just a tired woman, but a stranger to all, an event without precedent in the recent history of the district.

Collitt called Hiawatha Longfellow to his side, and the young apprentice mustard grower, having already foreseen his employers need, appeared at his side with the flask of mustik. Collitt took a moment to exchange a warm smile with his precious sidekick, not a patronising smile that speaks of rank and caste, but a genuine expression speaking volumes on the subject of the love between this surrogate father and son.

"Would ye run to the library and tell Mister Trimble to put on his town criers hat and tell the village" Collitt asked of the lad. Just about bursting with pleasure at being given such an important role in the drama unfolding in the market square, Hiawatha nodded briefly and sped off down Ur Street towards Clae Manor.

The infrequent need of a town crier meant that Ballentine Trimble rarely donned his crier's hat, but from his study window he spotted the approach of a breathless Hiawatha. Guessing a news item was awaiting broadcast, he reached for his tricorn and bell and greeted the lad on the steps. As Hiawatha told him of the arrival of the stranger, Ballentine began to ring his handbell.

People in the market place and in the alms houses on Ur Street heard the ringing and started unhurriedly toward the Library, as the Clae Manor was called when mentioned in the same sentence as the sensitive Mister Trimble. Ballentine made his leisurely way towards the market square. When the stragglers had been given due time to bunch in with the rest of the younger or more eager nucleus of the crowd, the bell ceased its summons, and every ear strained to hear the news.

"Oh yayerz, oh yayerz" whispered Ballentine "Hear ye

citizens of Clae, on this day we are visited by a stranger"

Miss Desdemona Pippin, who lived in the last alms house in the square, number thirteen, relayed the message in clear unerring tones to those too far back or too hard of hearing for Trimble's whispers to reach.

"A mysterious stranger in the village" she said

Athena Slough, an apprentice distiller in her early twenties and in possession of the kind of beauty usually found only in those fortunates born of Asian descent. Dark of eye and hair, but light of heart, Athena instantly picked up on Desdemona's innocent ad-lib, and had no fear of asking;

"What's so mysterious about this stranger then?"

"Well" replied Miss Pippin with a smile that signalled impending humour, and made her look coy "Any stranger round these parts is mysterious aint it?"

Indeed this was the case. No record of any visiting traveller existed for the last forty odd years, forty downright peculiar years by common standards.

The crowd that had gathered to hear the news now started down Ur Street to greet the mysterious stranger. Led by Ballentine Trimble like a pied piper in his tri-cornered hat, and Hiawatha Longfellow, strutting along beside him still enjoying fame by association.

The aptly named Mavis Stranger still sat on the packing crate that Collitt Semper had provided, but now that a good half cup of Mustik had passed her lips and made nonsense of perspective, she felt even less sure of her ability to rise than when she only had exhaustion to contend with. More baffling still was the sudden arrival of two dozen or so people, led by the pied piper, and staring at her with Frank Curiosity.

Frank Curiosity always put his stall next to Collitt Semper's, and then along with William Absurd, the trio made a lark of market days with ribald banter and much passing of the flask. Collitt's mustard and flowers, Frank's herbs, and William's vegetables were all arrayed facing the churchyard and latrines on the north side of the square.

Mavis Stranger, however, was amazed at the attention of which she was currently the centre, and felt panic welling inside her. Desdemona saw the signs of disquiet and began to usher the crowd back to a respectful distance, whilst turning her ten megawatt midwife smile on Mavis, a smile guaranteed to unravel the nerves of even first time mothers in the early stages of labour.

Relaxing had never been easy for Mavis, but under the glare of such powerful benevolence, the concrete resolve of her tension crumbled into a warm puddle of Mustik resting in the pit of her stomach, and as any citizen of Clae could point out, mere concrete is no match for the power of that particular tipple, so her resolve dissolved. Under the influence of this unexpected feeling of well being, that smacked of nostalgia and childhood summers, Mavis Stranger began to smile, and then to chuckle, not the kind of light laughter that follows in the wake of disposable wit, but the kind that turns age wrinkles into laughter lines, melts the years of aging and seeks to illuminate a face from within, by putting a small sun in the infinity of both pupils.

The concerned trio, in delight at such a rapid shift in her mood began to laugh along, even Ballentine Trimble's head bobbed up and down as he fought to retain his good humour within his girdle of hush.

Desdemona, as good natured as ever, but beginning to dwell on practicalities, realised that Mavis would need a proper place to rest. Ballentine's mood solved the problem for her, and she decided that he would offer the weary Stranger a refuge in the form of one of the furnished, but unused, rooms in the former manor house.

As Ballentine strolled happily toward the library with Mavis Stranger leaning on his arm, the onlookers began to become a market crowd again. Everyone that is except Miss

Pippin and Frank Curiosity, these two watched the departing pair with speculative thoughts betrayed by the look that passed between them, but it was Desdemona who put those thoughts within the limited confines of her vocabulary, when she said;

"Looks like old Bally Trimble might not be lonesome in his old age after all".

Frank just chuckled.

Chapter Two

Thirty miles away at the front entrance to the Coltsfoot and Briar Building Society, a young man lurked uncomfortably in the Monday shambles, nervously stealing glances at the activity within, although anybody who bothered to look at him would no doubt spot that his intention was to steal far more than glances.

Raiding the Coltsfoot and Briar Building Society was not the sort of thing that Dean Baxter usually did on a Monday morning, or any building society on any day of the week for that matter. In fact, the odd magazine liberated from the local corner shop had previously been the extent of his criminal activity, and that hardly counts because the owner of said corner shop, Mister Chandra, who came originally from poverty in Assam, was too shrewd not to notice, but too kind to take any legal action.

Dean, had recently parted company with his girlfriend, a quiet young woman named Sally, who worked on the checkout at the local supermarket. It had been said that Sally would be unlikely to win fame for her incisive intellect, but it is also true that she had kindness and honesty enough to give Dean Baxter a chance when no other woman would even look twice at him, and intelligence enough to spot the unsavoury changes in her boyfriend after he developed an interest in survivalist magazines and the local gun club; This particular hobby and its effect on young Baxter's weak and impressionable mind, resulted in mayhem at "Picking's Packing Company" with a staple gun and a second rate Clint Eastwood impersonation. An unwise antic which resulted in a workmate stapled by his overalls to a toilet door, a foreman reluctant to sit down, and a consequent vacancy at Picking's Packing Company. Life had certainly been unfair to Dean Baxter, as Dean Baxter saw it, and this was his plan to redress the balance; a half formed plan to commit an armed robbery, using a .357 magnum handgun stolen from the gun club's treasurer, also known to Baxter as Uncle Norman.

Here we are then, on the pavement, surreptitiously peeking in at the activity around the teller nearest to the door, and now we see Baxter reach in to his right hand jacket pocket to pull out a stocking, which he hurriedly pulls over his head, wincing as a particularly angry pimple yields to the nylon mesh. Now the handgun is produced from the waistband of his tracksuit trousers as he pulls on the door handle where the sign says PUSH, he panics momentarily, realises his mistake, and pushes his way inside.

A mere five minutes later, although, for Baxter, with fear and adrenalin pumping in his system, each of those tiny minutes dragged by as slowly as if he had spent them sitting on a cooker hob, he ran from the building clutching the gun and a small nylon backpack stuffed with notes. He ran to the corner and turned right into the alleyway where, half an hour earlier, he had parked his moped (the getaway vehicle) but it was gone.

It was at this point that he realised that the adrenalin coursing through his arteries earlier had been as butterflies in the tummy, compared to the throat-tightening, bladder-loosening, waves of heart stopping terror that washed over him now. He stared wildly about himself, praying that the moped had been moved, not stolen. Unfortunately for him the machine in question was at that moment in the hands of two rather more experienced thieves, who had, with opportunistic ease, taken his moped to the common for a little scrambling in preparation for the day when puberty would arrive to elevate them to the lofty status of teenage thugs.

Upon realising his situation, the hand of abject terror tightened its grip on his stomach. One simple command forced its way to the front of his mind to wrestle briefly with the tattered remains of his common sense, before taking control; the command was "RUN AWAY".

He began to run down the alley toward the high street, pulling the stocking from his head as he ran. At the far end of the alleyway, by the newsagent, he could see a ray of hope and without a second thought, which was probably just as well, considering how bad the first thought was, his lips pressed together and his jaw rigid in the fashion of grim determination, he set off in the direction of his only chance.

Chapter Three

Ten minutes or so earlier, Ma Mason, as she liked to be known, had looked out of her window to see if the young lodger had finished loading his old Ford van, still displaying the faded legend of its previous life as a commercial enterprise, providing the protein and calorific needs of late night revellers. The faded lettering along the side panels read 'Lucky Sid's Chip's and Kebab's', traditional fare with the chilli sauce so hot that the customers would apostrophise as much as the sign writer had done. He had been staying for eight months and, despite her reservations about him when he had first arrived on her doorstep, wearing tatty jeans, long hair and a shy smile she had enjoyed the company of this easy going young man. She sighed, more than a little sorry to see him go. She knew already that she would miss the sound of his guitar as he strummed gentle melodies in the evenings, and his cheery smile every morning as he set off to seek employment, and that same smile when he returned at midday, always unsuccessful in his efforts. He was good company and a good friend to Ma Mason these past months, and now he had finally given up hope of finding long term work in this town. Paying his bills and raising a small stake with a short term contract as a labourer at a building site, he had handed her notice of his intention to leave with obvious regret. He had no desire to once more accrue credit with the understanding and very trusting, Ma Mason.

As he loaded the last item, his guitar, into the van, he turned to smile at the landlady's face in the window. This was the moment he had been dreading, because he was as fond of Ma Mason as she was of him. Not just for the way she would sit in rapturous silence whenever he played his guitar, or even the way she defended him when the neighbours made barbed comments about "Her pet Hippy". No, the real pleasure had been in their friendship, made possible by her open and enquiring mind, a rare commodity in anyone, and virtually a miracle from a cross generation perspective. In return he had gained intimate knowledge of the 'doings' of her relations and the activities of her early life.

The past few months had taken their toll on Dylan as he had worked extremely hard on the building work, returning each evening to a hot meal and hot bath, not always in that order but never together. He had also been paying his way, which was a good feeling, and the pleasant evenings he spent with Ma Mason had also immersed him in a feeling of familial warmth.

As the end of the building work approached, there was little to keep him in the area, now that he could clear the credit that Ma Mason had extended to him for his room and board, and having bought a van from the irrepressible Lucky Sid.

At last he had the means to repay the money he owed and before he could relapse into debt, with a few hundred in his pocket and a tank full of fuel it was the time to move on in search of adventure.

On the doorstep Ma Mason gave him a hug, and said goodbye, both turning quickly away to hide the suspicious moisture gathering in their eyes. As he walked to his van, he heard the front door close, and felt a little tug at his heart as he mentally bade farewell to the first house that he had ever thought of as home.

From behind her net curtains, Ma Mason could see him climb behind the steering wheel of his old van, she watched him put on his seat belt, and heard the familiar rumble of the old engine reluctantly firing up once more. She saw him look one last time at the house, and she fancied that there were tears in his eyes.

"Daft young sod" she muttered, smiling as she dried her own eyes and watched him drive away.

Thus, Peter Lipton, known to most as Dylan, not after the singer as he would have preferred, but the guitar playing rabbit on the children's television programme *The Magic*

Roundabout, leaves his home and enters a pattern of events far different from anything he had imagined.

The engine of the Volkswagen tended toward sluggish in the first few miles of any journey, so it was with a little irritation that Dylan saw the traffic lights on the high street turn red. He started to slow down, hoping to avoid having to stop dead and have the engine stall, but as he got to the zebra crossing a young desperado hurtled out of an alley and on to the crossing, Dylan reacted immediately by reducing the vans speed from a crawl to a standstill, and the engine stalled. He tried the ignition once and nothing happened, he tried it a second time, this time the engine fired, but at the same moment the passenger door opened, and the young desperado sprang into the passenger seat in one awkward flail, tried to slam the door and bellowed with pain at the same moment, pulling his leg in to the van favouring his freshly barked shin. Without his leg in the way he could close the door properly, then turning his attention and a gun toward Dylan, breathlessly ordering him to drive. The gun being all the persuasion Dylan required to convince him, he drove.

The road he was on, Dylan realised, would take them out of town fairly rapidly and in to countryside, unless he could cross the river bridge and head off in the direction of one of the larger towns. He realised that if he didn't cross the bridge his chances of rapid rescue were slim to say the least. Although not a local by birth, Dylan had heard enough tales of wild and mysterious hills and woods out in this direction. He wanted to avoid them but the next villages were miles away. As he realised how grim the situation appeared to be, he noticed some construction work in progress at the river bridge and suddenly the situation took a turn for the worse.

"Damn" he muttered softly but with a great deal of passion "What the hell are they doing to the river?"

Dean Baxter the desperado was so lost in his world of paranoia and fear that he began to reply without thinking;

"They're making flood defences while the...." he suddenly seemed to recall the circumstances of his being there and changed his tone and tack, quite a deft manoeuvre when successfully executed in mid sentence. Sadly this was not such an occasion; "...shut up and stay on this road"

The town dissolved into countryside within a very few miles, and as the expected police pursuit failed to materialise, Baxter began to struggle down from fever pitch to a milder form of extreme agitation. Dylan was beginning to unwind slightly after the initial shock, and then, realising that Baxter had put the gun in his lap instead of waving it about like a flag at a carnival, he decided his life was not immediately threatened and felt it was time to find out a little about his predicament.

"Where are we going?" he asked casually, whilst pointedly keeping his eyes fixed on the horizon. Baxter made no immediate response, and it flashed across Dylan's mind for an instant that it was as if he was thinking about it for the first time, but people didn't just hijack campers on impulse, did they ?. At last the desperado spoke.

"Keep on this road until you see a sign for Lower Treaton, you can turn off there. Keep going along that road until I tell you what to do"

Silence fell between them for the time it took the camper to negotiate the route described by Baxter.

"Now turn right at the next chance" he said suddenly pointing to the turning with the gun and emphasising his message by shouting "There...there" Dylan reluctantly steered the vehicle off the surfaced road and on to a path in a state of advanced decay. The aged and weather beaten condition of vehicle and track took a rapidly fatal toll on the Volkswagen's moving parts and barely were they out of sight of the main road, when it crunched then squealed and ground to a final undignified halt.

Baxter regarded Dylan with contempt

"What now?" he snapped, as if Dylan had been the malicious architect of all the problems in Dean Baxter's life.

"It's dead" replied Dylan frankly "You killed my van" he added in tones tinged with regret.

"You missed the bloody turning" grunted Baxter looking back along the way they had come.

"What road is this then?" Dylan asked

Although less nervous than the would-be Jesse James, Dylan had been nervous enough to mistake a gap in the hedge on the left, for the indicated turning on the right, and had cut his own short route through a patch of woodland covering what was once the only path to Clae.

"I don't know where the hell we are" muttered Baxter with resignation "Still, at least we can't be seen from the road from in here"

Dylan surveyed the terrain with a growing sense of despair, wondering what was going on, and what part he was to play in the plans of the adolescent outlaw.

"Have you got a tent in here?" Baxter asked, looking with disapproval at the scattered memorabilia, freshly strewn across the floor of the camper. Dylan nodded gravely, as he scanned the turmoil for a clue as to where the tent may have ended up.

Within minutes, the unhappy duo were setting off towards an old deserted village that Baxter had heard tell of as a child. As he marched Dylan along at gunpoint, he told him where they were going. Poor Dylan had the tent on his shoulders, a gun at his back, and now he finds out that they are heading for the bomb shattered remains of a village, that nobody has been near for half a century. He was also regretful of having to leave his guitar and clothes back in the van.

"Sounds wonderful" he muttered, with undisguised irritation.

Typically, the vindictive young Baxter, noting his companion's fall in morale decided to press the point.

"They say the place is haunted, by the ghosts of all the villagers killed by the bomb during the war, and people have seen and heard strange things in these woods"

At this, Dylan brightened up, and started asking about the village and its sepulchral citizenry, but the topic was depressing Baxter, not only because it had failed to frighten the hippy, but more to do with the fact that he had indeed heard stories about the place, and he didn't want to be there, especially not with some long haired freak who actually liked the idea of meeting ghosts.

"What's the name of this place that we're heading for?"

Clae

he asked brightly

Baxter scowled at his back.

"Clae" he said "I think it was called Clae"

Chapter Four

Ballentine Trimble reclined in his tatty overstuffed armchair, and regarded Mavis with a changed perspective. When she had limped in to the market place that morning, the crowd had been fussy and sympathetic, and Mavis had been meek in her acceptance of their attention. Now, however, this same woman had been transformed, and yet the transformation had been fuelled by nothing more startling than an hour's rest, a touch of face powder, and a glass or two of the stuff that cheers (But renders you incapable of walking unaided).

Transformed from what, into what? You may ask, but even Bally Trimble could not put his finger on the exact nature of the metamorphosis. Perhaps, just a little more poise, maybe a glint of steel behind her eyes, but he finally decided that the shift was one of desperation through to inspiration.

"What brought ye to Clae then?" he asked, quietly with a smile.

Mavis looked at him from where she was perched primly on the front edge of the other armchair. She seemed, momentarily, to wrestle with something emotional and then to settle the internal conflict. Making confident eye contact with Ballentine, and yet in similar tones to the hushed reverence of his own voice, Mavis Stranger, told her story.

It's possible that Mavis is unique in the way she felt trapped by her sense of responsibility to her family and lifestyle, but you and I can freely doubt that. It could be that she saw something she recognised in the words of H.D. Thoreau when he spoke of "Most men" leading, what he described as "Lives of quiet desperation", and even though she understood the statement, and didn't seek to argue with it, she did notice what the passage neglected to say. After all, if most MEN feel desperation, despite the evidence of recorded history intimating that the male of the species has stacked the deck in his own favour, how much more inherent desperation must there be in the life of women who accept the strictures of acceptable behaviour as defined by a society that defies the individual seeking to abdicate the role in which they have been unwillingly cast. And how much quieter must they remain to protect that fragile stability called the family, when the children she bears and nurtures, elicit parental reflexes, which men are encouraged, even trained, to atrophy and repress.

This iniquity weighed down on her soul through years of marriage, not just because men appear to have an easier passage through life, but because society allows men the luxury of discontentment, while the women are expected to fulfil the role of stoic uncomplaining mother, even after the decree absolute, re-releases the father in to, relatively, carefree bachelorhood.

She even had the temerity, at times, to wonder if the exhaustion and boredom, which can be the mainstay of the housewife's existence, are as easily accepted as those husbands seem to imagine (If they are even aware of such) when they stop work for the day at early evening and take it for granted that the house will be clean and tidy (despite the natural ability of children to make this an improbable aim) expecting food to be stocked up in fridge and pantry, a hot meal ready to be served to them, and then, while he rests in his armchair, call his wife away from the washing to answer a child's cry from the bedroom, (Because he's been at work all day and far too tired for such banal domestic concerns) small wonder that it was mother for whom the child cries.

Now people, of both sexes, don't allow me to give you an inaccurate impression of Mavis as a feminist, along with all that your own experiences may associate with the term. Allow her to transcend such labels, and picture her instead as an intelligent individual with a little humanitarian fervour on behalf of the people who suffered the indignities of a situation not of their choosing, as she has, with nothing to sustain her, but the dream of a future which offers more freedom, and if not for her, then for other, future generations.

It is worthy of note, that she saw the pattern of her circumstance as an initial symptom of the changes that would eventually improve the lot of people such as she.

Some of you may point out that not all men and women are like Mavis and her husband, she would agree, and bless those fortunates, whilst empathising with the men and women who experience the same desperation, even when they can appear to have far less justification.

When Mavis was about eighteen, she finally realised with a dramatic sense of foreboding, that those who loved her, had certain expectations. She began to notice with dismay, that the morning dew of youth was evaporating, and stealing the bright jewels out of the gossamer of her dreams, leaving only a grey web strung taut between her desires and responsibilities.

Those she loved had plotted a course for her, and it seemed that spurning this social predestiny would risk losing that love which, for as long as she could remember had shielded her from the jagged edges of life.

Although Mavis had allowed herself to be carried along through the traditional rites of marriage and childbirth, the situation was not entirely unpleasant, for she loved her husband

and the three children they had raised, but the difficult thing to accept was the fact that she had relinquished choices, all the more difficult when the architect of her benign prison daily mocked her from behind the wrinkles on that face in the mirror.

Sometimes, when the insidious "What Ifs" were active, they could burrow and dig until they began to undermine the foundations of fortress "Responsibility"

As she denied and sublimated her fantasies, so they persisted, despite the impression that every year of wedlock and every child, alienated her further from her purest desires.

Fifteen years ago, her husband had ultimately resigned his own alchemical struggle to transmute the leaden dross of drudgery and boredom into the solid gold of his dreams, when he relapsed into eternity to become a naturalised citizen of the undiscovered country.

Mavis had mourned and mourned again as her remaining family was fragmented by marriage; moving on to begin their own families. How she wished she had told them of the coward she had been, when she was too young and too weak to blow a raspberry at convention, thumb her nose at her destiny, and beat an individual path through life. How she wished she had told them it was at least possible and at best desirable, to live your dreams or die striving. She knew, of course, that love shackled her to her present lifestyle and love had sealed her lips, in case her children heard and understood the advice, and took flight with their own fantastic hopes and desires.

Loneliness was the spectre she had shaped her life to avoid, fear of loneliness had bound her to her own parents' hopes for her, and then to her husband, and with his passing, her children. Then at last she had come to be alone, as she had feared, the spectre was every bit as devastating as she imagined it to be.

In the past few years, Mavis had seen grandchildren arrive, bringing with them an awakening for their parents, as the fact of their own mortality became undeniable. But even this new wisdom did not prevent them from mistakenly perceiving her potential as limited to the role of mother and grandmother.

A glossy brochure arrived in the post, and would quickly have joined its fellows in the waste-bin, had not the accompanying letter been from her oldest daughter. Despite her reservations, Mavis carefully read the pamphlet with a growing sense of betrayal.

The colour photographs showed a country house, converted into "flatlets" in the Middle Treaton Retirement accommodations, the text trotted out expansive lies about the fulfilling program of activities and the constant medical care on hand to prolong the nonexistence within those quaint walls. As she understood the implications of her daughter's letter, her heart broke.

It had spoken of her children's concern for her, how lonely she must be, and how much easier they would feel if she was somewhere that would ensure her continued well being.

Mavis had wept at first, then she had cursed before finally, she succumbed to despair, in the throes of which, she even contemplated surrender, then she withdrew inside herself.

With Mavis-the-wife-mother-grandmother out of the way, Mavis the unfettered child, jumped at her long awaited opportunity to seize the reigns and take flight. First she went to Middle Treaton Retirement Accommodations, to peer through the railings at the old and infirm, to know for certain that, she would never be old enough to live in such a place, even if she lived to be one hundred and twenty three.

Then she had walked, dazed, through Lower Treaton and beyond, until she was lost, tired and miles from any road or path. Only then as darkness fell did the older Mavis step back out of the shadows and begin to panic.

The following morning, after a sleepless and terrified night of aimless struggle she had stumbled in to the market at Clae and caught up with herself in an overstuffed armchair, with a cup of Mustik rapidly and permanently dissolving the divide between the old and new Mavis, forging a new being in the crucible of adversity, and giving a candid summary of her life to the dignified and attentive person of Ballentine Trimble.

By midday the market was almost crowded with the bulk of Clae's population haggling and exchanging goods. Even the more reclusive residents would venture into the heart of the village on market days; people as enigmatic as the bee keeper, a man infamous as a master of epic reticence and rumoured to be high in the ranks of the Black Coven.

In such a small village it may be expected that all business is communal, and it is true that with a grapevine that could shame the telephone system into voluntary redundancy, news is as common as privacy is scarce. Even so, the secrecy of the Black Coven remained intact and unchallenged, primarily because nobody wanted to know anything about its nocturnal activity in the orchards that formed the north eastern boundary of Clae.

The villagers knew of the bee keeper who appeared at the market to trade his honey and wax, which were both indispensable commodities. The honey used to aid the production of mustik and the wax produced the candles that flicker in the late evening, as people gather to drink and exchange stories and ideas about the bee keeper and the orchard manager, who is equally enigmatic, and who also lives a solitary life in the privacy of the orchards.

One of the reasons for the mystery surrounding these two is the time honoured tradition of the scrumping season. At the right time of year when fruit hangs heavy on the trees, the villagers scamper en masse to pick the fruit, then dry it, cook it, make it into pies and jams and generally, to eat and preserve as much as possible, to see them through the winter. At this festival time of the year, the orchards are overrun and every inch is thoroughly scoured for nuts and berries, and yet, nobody ever sees hair nor hide of the two reclusive residents.

Speculation about these two unusual but vital members of the community, places them high up in the equally mysterious Black Coven, which meant that they were untroubled by visitors. Of the two, only the bee keeper would steal into the market to trade, and on these occasions, he would waste no time on pleasantries or small talk, merely conducting his barter then slipping quietly back to the orchards. Often, when he came to the village, he would also bring carved wooden utensils to trade. These items, always highly prized for their practical elegance, were assumed to be the handiwork of the orchard manager, carved from the dead wood he cleared when he wasn't attending to the welfare of his deciduous brethren.

Burma Conduit was named from the books in the library according to tradition but in her case, the Bard of Avon had been overlooked, as a source, in favour of an atlas, and an electrician's handbook. By Clae standards, Burma is an old maid.

Nearly thirty years old and unmarried, she is apprenticed to her parents, the vegetable farmers of Clae, William Absurd in the south, and his estranged wife, Ophelia Luckett in the north. They parted company for the purely practical convenience of living on the land that each of them farmed, the marriage being of no great concern having served its purpose by producing Burma. Burma manages to keep in good favour with both parents by taking Ophelia's produce to market and by selling it from William's barrow. She also makes time to keep herself happy by teaching the handful of young that the people of Clae managed to produce. Her school is at the Manor house in one of the many uninhabited rooms. Her text books are from Ballentine's library rooms, and through her efforts, the largely redundant skills of reading and writing, persist. Algebra trigonometry and the like, however, were sensibly classified as black arts, and thus, not included in the informal curriculum.

On this particular market day, the humourless and yet

formidable, Ophelia Luckett made an unexpected appearance. At least, Uther Smith was not really expecting to turn quickly and suddenly be face to face with her. Uther was surprised to the point of shock, not merely because Ophelia is formidable and rarely smiled, but because she usually stayed at the farm, and allowed her daughter, Burma, to represent her at market.

As one of the respected elders of the community, Uther has responsibilities beyond merely running the distillery, including the welfare of the people and property of Clae. It is in this capacity that he had come to fear the arrival of Ophelia and her brusque manner, undiluted by the respect which was awarded him by most citizens, except the bee keeper, Desdemona and the unimpressible Ophelia Luckett.

Although it is true that she rarely smiled, Ophelia is not as formidable as she seems to Uther but, as usual, before he could muster his composure, it fled, and he began making noises in his throat like pauses without words between them.

"Ah......Um.......Oh........Err........Um...Ah." he gibbered, looking about him for some source of moral or physical support. Ophelia marked time by rolling her eyes in impatient irritation until Uther recalled the fundamentals of verbal communication. In desperation Uther glanced in the direction of William Absurd's barrow, to make a silent plea, in the form of an expression a spaniel would be proud to wear when begging for food. William, however, sensibly conversant with his weakness in dealing with either his estranged wife or his friends pathos, had made a tactical withdrawal, as revealed by the back of his head currently scampering to the churchyard and the sanctuary of the toilets. Even the faces of Frank Curiosity and Collitt Semper were treacherously turned away from him seemingly engrossed in the difficult task of arranging their wares, as if presentation of stock made a difference to traders without competitors.

Thus abandoned to his fate, Uther reluctantly returned his attention to the matter in hand, and met the unflinching gaze of Ophelia's dark Gallic eyes with all the confidence of a small rodent facing a cobra.

"Well?" demanded Ophelia, making sure that Uther's concentration was pointed in the same direction as his eyes.

"Well" he replied quietly as he reluctantly relinquished hope of running after William and hiding in the toilet, because of the loss of face he would incur.

"Well, what's to be done about the cottages?" she demanded, "I told ye two years ago that they were damp, and what have ye done about it? I'll tell ye, not a blessed thing"

When Fulmin Pinnock XII self declared Emperor of Clae and protector of the west paddock, had lived in the manor house, his estate had included some land, including the west paddock, that he protected, and the mews cottages standing on its perimeter. With his demise, the estate had been divided up according to communal need, thus the cottages now housed the workers for the land managed by Ophelia, but the west paddock, known locally as Pinnock's paddock, had always been a bog, and year by year the rising water level reduced the cottage gardens to quagmire, and now the dampness began to seep in to the walls of the buildings themselves.

This is not an easy situation to deal with, even for the philanthropic Uther, when building materials are scarce and building skills scarcer still. Housing in Clae is a finite resource, and as such demand maintenance. The only spare accommodation is in the manor house with its many furnished but uninhabited rooms.

Uther often felt the weight of his responsibility to the village, but never so acutely as when there was a strong woman around to underscore the ethical implications of his lofty status. It must be said that strong women always frighten Uther, even his apprentice, the strong willed, Athena Slough, who's willowy physique and soft brown eyes belied the sheer unbending steel of her resolve when fighting for a principle. He secretly suspected that Desdemona had covertly recruited Athena as apprentice, so that in due course she would hold dual office as head of the distillery and matriarch of Clae. It is a credit to Uther's intelligence that he was absolutely correct, Desdemona did indeed guide the zeal of Athena's sense of justice in respect of the day that Desdemona herself could no longer champion equanimity.

It remained a mystery to everyone why Emperor Pinnock should proclaim himself protector of the most worthless tract of land within the confines of the Clae hills, but being one of the late Emperor's more innocuous eccentricities nobody thought much about the paddock until the flooding began to encroach on the cottages.

Now the problem was very much in the sweaty hands of a stricken Uther Smith, who could not break away from his eye contact with Ophelia despite his head moving from side to side. He was convinced that if for once he could break eye contact, he would be able to speak.

Ophelia, noting the subsidence in this pillar of the community, allowed him a respite.

"I shall expect to hear from the council of elders about this matter, afore next market day" she said releasing Uther from his trance by turning on her heel and vanishing into the throng.

Clae

Chapter Five

Ballentine and Mavis sat in companionable silence as the afternoon sun made subtle alterations to their features, exposing previously unnoticed aspects of each other's physiognomies. The two O'clock sunlight had clear access to both faces, no room for shadow, like a tableau illustrating their open hearted honesty. Three O'clock came with some shade and highlights to give expression to the depth of their compassion, and so on through the afternoon until the sun sank low on the horizon and cast its last amber shafts into the library at such an angle, that each discerned a darker side in the other. Through these changes, they have observed the silent unfolding of the other's personality and remained enchanted, until early evening brings a sense of kinship beyond the mere facts of their lives and actions, an understanding based on the evidence of their souls outpouring through the expressions of natural light.

Ballentine was astounded that anyone as intelligent and spirited as Mavis obviously is could be written off as a spent resource by any society (other than one on the brink of devouring itself in a frenzy of avarice). The fact that he found her attractive was more a matter of personal taste, although he mentioned it anyway, and saw that inner light again melt away the years. It was at that moment that he determined that he should make it his pleasure to cause that light to shine in her eyes as often as he could.

Mavis for her part was charmed and disarmed by this softly spoken, genteel librarian with his passion for the books and encyclopaedic memory which would have overawed her, had not his idiosyncratic nature, reassured her of his humanity.

From the very fabric of their differences, and the depths of their diversity, was a bond forged that was a process of holistic fusion, and it was with complete assurance that Ballentine excused himself to prepare only one bed, for them both, that evening.

It was then, while Ballentine was out of the room, as Mavis rested in the snug security of a shared affection, that she heard the voice. Ballentine had described the way he could hear the books, and his hushed respect for the written word, but she had assumed that the observation was metaphoric, and not nearly as real as the deep, vibrant tones issuing from the direction of the book case. At first she had thought it to be Ballentine joking with her, and then she had realised that the voice was different, somehow sylvan. By the time she recognised the inhuman, sylvan quality of the voice, she was absorbed in what it was saying, too intrigued to be unnerved by it.

"Woman" rumbled the disembodied voice "Listen carefully to me, be sure ye understand my words, because I do not care to repeat myself"

Mavis nodded her understanding, then realised that ghostly voices may not notice a nod, so she addressed the bookshelf and said,

"I am listening, go ahead"

The rich male voice (perhaps the books talking, as Ballentine believed) made a slightly disgruntled sound as if it had expected a more dramatic reaction from her than just puzzled interest. Although it continued with its grand soliloquy, there was still an irritated edge to it.

"Be aware" it said "That two more strangers are coming to the village. One of them is a man of peace and of no danger, the other is a man of violence and he is to be avoided at first."

"At first?" queried Mavis puzzled.

"Yes" said the voice "At first. All this will become clear"

Mavis sat and listened while the voice spoke of omens and portents. As it faded away it said something about the coven, which did succeed in sending an excited shiver of fear down her spine, and then she was alone in the silence, that roars in the wake of strange events.

Ballentine returned to find Mavis looking quizzically at the bookshelves, he guessed what had transpired in his absence, and asked Mavis what she had heard. In her gratitude for his understanding, which erased her doubt, she candidly revealed what she remembered of the conversation with the books. He, for his part, listened thoughtfully until she had concluded, then with a pause for the reassurance he broadcast with his grin, he swept his tri-corn hat from its stand, and walked briskly out of the room.

From the comfort of the armchair, and the quiet of her contentment, Mavis heard the sound of the town criers bell, growing quieter as he travelled down Ur Road, in the direction of the village square.

Having fulfilled his duty as town crier, Ballentine went back to the library and to Mavis, where he relinquished the dismal future of solitude he had previously thought awaited him, and where Mavis at last let go of her late husband, and began to live for her own sake, with hope, joy, anticipation, but most of all, with Ballentine Trimble, who was the vindication of her optimism, the ability she had for putting her faith in the realm of tomorrow, the domain where all dreams are realised.

Most mornings, in most of the country, as soon as they wake, the people dash from place to place, from home to work, and back again, from day to day, year after year, from birth to burial, and always by the fastest means at their disposal: Disposal being the keystone of this social chapter, and verse the only acceptable soap box from which to air dissent.

    The village of Clae, however, knows nothing of such things and usually sleeps soundly, easing gently into each new day, waking as some people wake, with first a blending of dreaming and reality (whatever that is), in those rare and beautiful moments when the dreamer is aware of their role in the fantasy, and can exercise some control over it; then comes a little awareness of the body parts as limb by limb the body responds to consciousness and the mind, once more attuned to the limitations imposed by the physical world, resumes its station at the helm.

    The people of Clae were its body parts, and the entity had its own life. Reborn each morning as its component citizens awoke one by one and began the celebration of existence which is the way of life in this place.

    When the church had gone and the toilets were built with the remains, it was decided to retain the bell, as an alarm. This required a bell tower, which was also constructed from the shattered ecclesiastic masonry, and added as a tasteful afterthought to the freshly built latrines.

    The bell, as I said, is an alarm, the voice of the village

entity, waking rudely to become suddenly aware of its peril, and crying out its distress. This morning was one of those rare occasions, with no time for the gradual easing in to a new day, for Clae screamed out impending danger from its stone larynx in the church yard; from this garden of the dead it cried CLANG, (AWAKE!)......CLANG, (DANGER!).......CLANG, (BEWARE!)......and so on until the people mustered in the manor house grounds, exchanging theories on the nature of their peril, and wondering how many other strange events would occur in this new era of experience.

    Ballentine was unsinkable that morning, and wore an expression of serene contentment even the ominous tolling of the bell could not hope to penetrate. A light of joy added lustre to his customary smile that rarely bothered to enlist the participation of his facial muscles, but contented itself with a wrinkling of his eyes in a delighted epicanthic fashion. Even so, he responded to the sound as rapidly as everyone else. Mavis, although unsure of what was happening, but unwilling to hinder him with questions, wordlessly followed his lead, so that both were ready to greet the first arrivals as they trudged up Ur road to the insistent cracked chiming of the bell.

    Mavis was also under the spell that had rendered her new love hopelessly smug, and unaware of the fragility of this social microcosm, as she was, she was not as infected by the urgency of the expanding crowd; to her this new excitement was another aperitif for the sensual banquet her life should be, so long as she dared to allow it.

The small crowd, chatting quietly and speculatively among themselves, braced themselves for the worst, while hoping for the best, but preparing to exercise the determination to do whatever they could about whatever disaster had befallen them.

The spring morning sun kindly lit them as they waited, as if to make the waiting easier, this effort on behalf of the elements was toasted in the traditional way thanks to the more terrestrial efforts of Uther Smith who thoughtfully paused on his way to pick up a jug of mustik, which passed among the crowd spreading good cheer, leaving in its wake a ripple of warmth in the places, despite its valiant effort, even the sun could not reach.

The bell ceased its noise.

The crowd stilled in anticipation.

As one they turned to face Ur road to see the approach of whoever had decided that they needed to be summoned.

Of the few who liked to dwell on the fringes of this hemline of civilisation, Shylock Giza, the miller, was perhaps the most sociable. Although living in relative isolation on the west boundary of Clae where the river Henry powered his mill before leaving the village, he would often venture to the square, for an evening drink, and to market to sell flour and bread.

Shylock, is easily underestimated because of his childlike candour and open handedness, but these were attributes he had been taught to cultivate, by the miller who had taught Shylock his trade many years ago, when Fulmin Pinnock had been a young man. The skills he had learned along with his trade were those required to understand and befriend children, to sort out petty squabbles and arguments, before they became feuds that grew as the children grew and reached such a size that they could cause a rift of such magnitude that a little place like Clae could be swallowed up and destroyed. He helped to forge the bonds by which a society can hold itself together in the face of tribulation.

Wherever he went, he would be followed by a small flock of children, all eager to sample one of his legendary pastries, or hoping he might entertain them with one of his impromptu puppet shows, the device by which he could convey his messages, tales with an ethic concealed within, although not too deeply hidden that it could be missed.

The love that the children have for the florid old man,

allows him to keep his finger on the pulse of their politics, and to guide their energies and help them shape their dreams to the patterns of thoughtfulness and altruism.

His love of the river and the mill, however kept him away from the hub of his universe, which suited Burma Conduit, because it allowed her time to teach the children those other, perhaps, secondary skills that they missed by trailing Shylock from place to place.

Despite this great trust that the citizens of Clae placed in him with their rare and thus particularly precious offspring, or maybe because of it, the speculation surrounding him, made him a member of the Black Coven, even if he had denied it. The legend of the coven was a thrill for the villagers, so even though no evidence was found, none was ever sought, mere gossip was sufficient in itself to keep children and adults away from the orchards where the coven was supposed to meet, and to fuel the stories told on cold winter evenings over a cup of Mustik.

But the man now striding closer was not the miller, or the puppeteer, or even the keeper of children's secrets. It was as keeper of the river that he strode onward, with perspiration beading the livid skin of his furrowed brow.

"LISTEN UP" He cried breathlessly, as soon as he thought he was audible, "LISTEN, THE RIVER HENRY IS DRY"

Shocked silence like a wall stopped him dead in his tracks as he caught his breath, and gratefully accepted a short swig from the jug. The people had expected bad news, but they had also expected to be able to do something about it. A fire could be fought, a barn could be rebuilt, a death could be acknowledged and the life of the deceased then celebrated. But this was a crushing blow, the river Henry; the aorta of Clae's heart had bled dry. With no water to sustain it the village would surely die.

The assembled crowdlet sauntered in a dispirited fashion to the square to see the Henry as it trickled behind the distillery where once it had flowed as if from creation to eternity.

Shylock Giza called out the gathering for hush, and coughed twice to ensure his voice did not break as he was breaking, and said,

"I've closed the sluices at the mill, so we have a small reservoir there, so I advise ye all to collect some water, to use until we sort this out."

Despite themselves they clung to this optimistic allusion and began half heartedly to rally.

"We can bottle as much as possible" cried Uther on behalf of his staff, able at last to direct his good eye toward Ophelia Luckett's unflinching glare, now that they both faced a problem from the same angle.

"Good" cried Desdemona rising to meet the challenge, "And make sure your water butts are cleaned and ready for the next rainfall we are blessed with"

Exactly how and from what direction hope had made an entrance into this scene I could not say, but fuelled by these desperate measures, hope was once again welcomed in the town where it wanted, one day, to retire.

Chapter Six

During the night, Dylan and Dean Baxter had found little to talk about, as they scrambled among old and well established brambles the size of saplings, hunting for the pass that Baxter was sure existed, having been convinced by local legend.

Dylan found he could only keep up his fear for so long, and with the passage of time he found his initial trepidation was transmuting into irritation, and dislike for Baxter. However, dislike was another thing he found hard to keep up, and soon lapsed into a kind of mildly terrified excitement, which he generated from the thoughts of the ghost village somewhere ahead. Even the woodland had started to take on a sepulchral glow of pre-dawn illumination, and more than once, the moonlight had given him a glimpse of a figure, silent and swift, moving between trees ahead of them, always from the corner of his eye, he saw it, and so allowed that it could have been his overdriven imagination, creating for his entertainment, a problem more to his taste than being forced through unchecked woodland growth at gun point.

Dean Baxter, for his part, was wallowing in self pity, as he searched for a way through or over the hills. He still brandished the firearm as if it were a certain credit card, saying more about him than cash ever can, but cash was the reason he had committed the robbery. With this thought he smiled coldly to himself, as if having money was more important than the means of acquiring it: as if his wealth could compensate for his criminality and the loss of his respect for himself.

With the burden of a firearm in one hand and a rucksack of cash in the other, Dean Baxter was finding progress harder than his hostage. He could no more hand the bag to Dylan to carry than he could contemplate handing the weapon to the other man, so he struggled on with thorns snagging the bag and his clothing working twice as hard as his captive and suffering twice the damage.

His one redeeming feature was the fact that somewhere in the artless void of his existence he had brushed with an ethical individual who had left him with the seeds of conscience, which sprouted tiny shoots of reason, enough to trouble him when they tried in vain to take hold in his soul, and where rootless and devoid of warmth they shrivel and laid dormant waiting.

Dylan began to see humour in his plight and found it subsequently difficult to suppress his new found diffidence toward the threat of the gun.

Baxter said nothing, for the most part unaware of his hostage, too wrapped in self pity to notice anything except the suffering he was enduring, and not just the bramble scratches and nettle stings that constantly dragged him back to his current situation, but the fact that his simple plan had gone so far awry was taking him to unplumbed depths of self that he would rather not explore, for fear of finding out how far below his potential he had fallen.

It was about the time that the clouds reflected the first stray rays of sun from their soft underbellies that they heard the sound of the displaced church bell in Clae. Both men stopped to better hear the sound they thought they could not have heard. Sure enough, there it was again in open defiance of their incredulity, the sound of a church bell from a dead village.

Baxter looked for some comfort or reassurance from Dylan, but the other man did not even notice the glance as he smiled inwardly in secret wonder at such an exciting impossible fact.

In darkness and confusion they eventually stumbled on the pass that Mavis had happened upon, without knowing, only a day before.

The pass, such as it is, can claim that title only by virtue of the fact that it is marginally more navigable than the surrounding hills. In daylight and with a good deal of luck on her side, Mavis had passed through with relative ease, reasonably unscathed: Dylan and Baxter, however had gone by a more treacherous method, although within feet of the route Mavis had used, the advantage of daylight was not with them and they could not make informed choices about such things as whether to move to the left of a particular bush to avoid a prodigious patch of mature nettles, or stroll easily past by the right. Consequently they were stung scratched and torn at until the sun was sufficiently high in the heavens to show them where they were in relation to these previously invisible pitfalls.

    The bell had stopped ringing by the time, Baxter and Dylan had cleared the trees that thickly coated the hills, and emerged on the west side of in the bowl of land that is Clae, beside the north bank of the dry bed of the river Henry. Ahead of them they could see the mill standing idle, its large paddle wheel static in the run, as if it hadn't turned in years.

    With both of them unsure of what lay ahead of them, they felt drawn together in a mutual trepidation, which has no knowledge of details such as liking one another, or not. It only chooses to be aware that both of them share in the situation, and for different reasons they both seek out the support of the only other human being. Baxter turns to Dylan because he had always sought a father/Teacher to guide him through the teeming confusions that constitute the life of a lad beaten by a father, who was beaten by his father. Dylan turns to Dean Baxter, though, because he is a naturally gregarious person always happy to exchange companionship, so in the face of this mysterious circumstance, he looked for support where he always looked for it, and consequently, usually found it, in the basic kindness of ordinary people. Even the simplicity of the conspiratal look that they exchanged, merely reiterating the fact that they were together in the situation just that simple look is the stuff of life to a philanthropic soul such as Dylan, and enough to sustain him through worse trials than the imagined terrors of a ghost town.

By silent agreement, they avoid the dead river, and the silent mill, by circling north, and thus they failed to notice the mill pond swelling slowly beyond the mill, where the last trickle of the Henry meets the closed sluices to form the last hopes of the village.

Ahead of the two adventurers lay cultivated fields, rows of ripening crops beckoning at the wind's whim. Beyond the fields etched in dark industrial shades against the pastel wash of morning sky, they can make out the shapes of the buildings around the village square, the squat houses, the ornate distillery and even the manor house at the point where the horizon becomes the land of cloud sculpture, barely concealing islands and mountain ranges, all of these forms had the aura of menace to Baxter, and the formless promise of mystery to Dylan.

As the buildings grew larger, they separated from the dark mass that distance depicted them, into individual dwellings with character and charm. A further enigma unfolded before their eyes; in the street outside the distillery, people were busy with an urgent task.

For an astrologist, there may be the evidence of strange planetary conjunctions to explain why Clae had such a spate of unusual activity. In the last two generations no visitor had entered Clae, and the river Henry had flowed strong and swift, if not cleanly, through the village. In the last two days however, there had been three visitors coinciding with the Henry running dry.

If superstition had ruled supreme in Clae, the population may have drawn the conclusion that there was an arcane relationship between the two events. These people did not generally look for primary causes or scapegoats. Apportioning culpability, they had long ago discovered, was a waste of time better spent discovering solutions. This methodology certainly increased the chances for survival.

It was Ben Caliban who saw the approaching strangers

first and alerted the others with a low mumble and a nudge. As the two interlopers drew close enough for conversation, the entire crowd of villagers was turned to face them falling rapidly into curious silence. Baxter's suspicious state of mind caused him to interpret it as the kind of sinister silence that greets Sherlock Holmes when he enters a pub on the moor in pursuit of the Hound of the Baskervilles.

Ben Caliban had also noted the gun being carried by Baxter. Even though Ben had never seen a gun, let alone fired one, he knew enough to recognise it for what it was and had some vague impression that somebody with malicious intent could hurt another with a thing like that.

Frank Curiosity encouraged the crowd to approach the new arrivals. Cautiously, remaining behind was Absurd, until even he was eventually pulled forward by a calculating and calculated glance from his estranged wife, Ophelia Luckett.

Baxter's consternation increased exponentially as the distance between them grew less: Eventually, unable to stand his tension any longer, he waved the gun in the direction of the crowd. If it had not been for the fact that he had manufactured his hardened image for the purpose of intimidating Dylan, he would have reacted in fright and fled the scene: But the raw adrenalin coursed so thickly through him that he could almost taste it on his fear dried tongue and his nerve balanced on a knife edge only as long as he had Dylan there to be tough in front of, feeding his image on Dylan's fear of it.

His sidelong glance at his captive revealed, however, no trace of concern. Instead, the hostage looked back at the stares of the crowd with their naked wonder reflected in his eyes.

Baxter, desperate to regain the upper hand struck at Dylan's face with the butt of the pistol, catching him a glancing blow to the bridge of his nose and in an arc upwards across his forehead. The suddenness of the attack, as much as the impact knocked Dylan off his feet and he reacted instinctively, gasping with pain and covering his face with cupped hands, fell and rolled into a foetal curl while he dealt with the waves of pain that crashed over him with their flecks of white heat that cavorted in his vision. Though his eyes remained squeezed shut to everything except the involuntary tears that flowed unnoticed down his cheeks.

Baxter turned to the crowd with a snarl and a smile of triumph. He had impressed even himself. The smile on his face froze when he noticed the change in the atmosphere. The benevolent curiosity he had mistaken for menace, had been replaced by a menace that could not be mistaken for anything less. These people had just witnessed an act of violence that was unequalled in their world; they were shocked and disgusted by the spectacle. Ben Caliban recognising the threat of the gun, held back the crowd with a relatively small hand gesture which Uther had upheld with a nod.

Baxter, thinking what to do next, fell back on some idea about the church being a place of sanctuary and demanded instructions on how to get there, punctuating and emphasising his demand by lightly kicking Dylan where he now lay on a pavement that resembled a Pollock nightmare due to the blood he was shedding.

The public toilet facility was the only thing that was left of the church. Uther Smith solemnly pointed at the latrines with its small gothic bell tower and shook his head sadly as the injured young man was half pushed and half kicked across the road by the vicious one, and out of sight into the building.

Uther was deeply torn between his need to save the village and his painful concern for the victim of the outrage. He looked in bewilderment at Desdemona Pippin who nodded gravely in sympathy and moved closer to him that they may talk.

"I dare say the lad will be alright for the minute, my dear. Ye do what ye need to do to save that water and we will both sort this out in time for supping"

Uther was visibly relieved by the suggestion and pausing only to kiss Miss Pippin gently on the cheek, began rallying the forces to begin bottling the pool of water that was once their beloved Henry.

As the village dispersed into the Mustik plant, and down to the mill pond, Desdemona smiled briefly at Uther's back, then gathered herself and looked at the toilets while her jaw set in jutting determination. She crossed the road and made her way towards the door by which the strangers had entered.

Chapter Seven

Baxter heard the door open and a woman's voice asking if she may come in. Baxter was still bewildered by having found a toilet instead of a chapel and raised the gun in the direction of the door. Desdemona stepped directly into the line of sight along the barrel of the magnum down to the face of terror at the other end.

"He needs seeing to" she said nodding at Dylan seated on the stone floor still cradling his face. Baxter nodded hesitantly as she came forward and opening a cabinet over the wash basins she took out a towel and wet it with some of the, now precious, fluid from the sink pushed it against Dylan's hands until he realised what it was and applied it himself to the gash on his head.

"Ye will live, I dare say" she said to Dylan in comforting tones. Then she turned to Baxter, "What are ye going to do?" she asked him. Baxter continued to target her with the weapon and seemed to be confronting the problem for the first time, which in fact he was.

"Ye will need food" she reminded him, walking to a cupboard set into the wall. "I can buy food" said Baxter reaching inside his backpack to pull out a few loose notes and fling them onto the floor. Desdemona stopped where she was and looked at them.

"What is it" she asked as she stooped to pick up one of them and turning it over she added "Where is the picture of the King" Then she dropped it back on the floor and shrugged "Not real money" she muttered as she continued towards the cupboard.

Baxter saw her reach for the door handle and shouted "Where are you going?" Desdemona stopped again and said "This is the broom cupboard, I am going to clean in here" Baxter stepped across the room and pushed her out of the way. He cautiously opened the door and saw only cleaning utensils, nodding his permission to continue he foolishly turned his back on the Matriarch of Clae.

The first he knew of his mistake was the broom handle that caught him squarely between the legs, a rapid blow that made him turn to face his assailant in time to catch the brush end of a besom, whistling as it cut the air, full slap across his cheek. A single shot amplified by the small stone room, seemed to shake the fabric of time. It was like slow motion the way that Baxter stared in disbelief at the gun falling from his hand, the way Desdemona Pippin stood her ground despite her conviction that she had been struck by lightning.

During the next few moments Baxter had fled his

sanctuary without further hindrance and also without his weapon or bag of loot, his hands clutching at his more highly prized but bruised valuables, eyes watering, he was gasping for breath. Nobody intercepted him.

This uncoordinated flight had occurred as Dylan had begun to look out from beneath the soothing cold towel and Desdemona Pippin flopped to the floor in a heap of skirt and scarf.

Uther Smith was the first to realise the implications of the gunshot, and was consequently the first to arrive at the scene. He rushed in without thought of injury and saw as he had feared; the Matriarch sprawled upon the floor. Rushing to her side and lifting her head to cradle it in his arm he listened to the sound of her breathing. "It's the old trouble" he declared. "Where is Athena?"

About then Miss Athena Slough had arrived at the scene and pushing past the onlookers she made her way to her mistress' side. With one hand she took over Uther's position at her head, with the other she offered passing comfort to Uther with a squeeze of his hand. She then indicated the audience with a nod in their direction: a message that Uther received immediately and responded to by beginning to clear the room.

It was at that moment Uther knew for certain that

Clae

Desdemona had groomed Athena to inherit her position. At that exact moment Uther also knew that she had chosen wisely.

Inside the toilets, Desdemona had been dosed with a few sips of Mustik and reassured that the bullet had missed her. The fright she had been caused by the noise of the gun had caused her considerable shock, a strain that was bordering on fatal. A doctor outside of Clae would have told her that she had a serious heart condition, and the worry of it may have been the death of her. Here in Clae she knew only that she had to make allowances for her advancing years, so that some of the activities she had enjoyed as a young girl must be replaced by other more suitable forms of enjoyment. The reality and inevitability of death was the reason she had taken the precaution of training a successor. Even so, today was not the day for Clae to acknowledge a new Matriarch. Desdemona was soon sitting up and smiling while Athena put her training to good use as she ministered to Dylan's needs by bathing his cuts and looking for other signs of injury.

Dylan was still rather dazed and could only manage a ghost of a smile as he let Athena examine him. It was only when she was finished that Desdemona told her to let Uther know that she was alright. Athena stepped outside to find Uther waiting with crippling concern for news of Miss Pippin. It was like seeing a sunrise on his face the way it brightened with the news. As it dawned on Uther, others read the expression and drew its obvious conclusion. As one they turned back to the Mustik plant and their work, satisfied that perhaps hope and luck were more than just good friends, they certainly seemed to be together today.

    Having solved the immediate problems, Athena was looking at Desdemona to see if there was anything else she needed to do. Miss Pippin for her part looked to Uther Smith to get her somewhere more suitable. This was good news for Uther, because he needed to be busy to combat his concern for his old friend and sparring partner, his Matriarch.

    Athena turned her attention back to Dylan who was clearly out of danger and feeling more curiosity than self pity. Questions gathered in on his lips which were pursed for the first interrogative.

    Athena knew that this was not the time for lengthy explanations because she too felt the need to be involved in the emergency threatening the village. Raising her hand to brush Dylan's hair away from the cut on his head she asked him:

    "How do ye feel?"

    Dylan raised his eyes to hers as she pulled from her overall pocket a strip of cloth with which she began to bandage his head.

"I think I will be fine" Dylan assured her as she expertly fixed the bandage without tape or safety pins. Athena nodded her approval of his attitude as she stepped back and offered her hand to assist Dylan to his feet. He accepted the proffered hand and was raised from the floor, but he winced as a pain behind his eyes throbbed suddenly, making his vision dim as a surge of nausea rose briefly and then ebbed with the pain to an almost tolerable background ubiquity.

Athena had observed the entire episode with two forms of concern. On the whole, her worry was that she may have been wrong about the injury being worse than it looked. Behind that, however, were thoughts about how interesting, brave and good looking this stranger was to her. She didn't want to discover that he was the kind to seek sympathy, so it was with some relief that she saw him master the sensations that assailed him as she led him by the hand out into the fresh air of the village square.

Abandoned goods and possessions littered the square where their owners had left to tackle the emergency, in the sure and certain knowledge that those things would be there later to retrieve. Athena explained to Dylan what was happening as they crossed the road to the distillery. Such a short explanation was required that Dylan found that rather than answering many of his questions, he was finding still more that begged to be asked. He allowed the abridged version of events to suffice in the light of the crisis, asking only if there was any way he could help. He was rewarded with a smile from Athena which, to Dylan, was like a caress. Thus charged, he was set to work in the bottling plant where he rubbed shoulders with the citizens of Clae in their time of greatest need. There was no need for any introductions because word spread rapidly and Dylan had his references on display, with a blood stained bandage around his head, his shirt grimy with sweat and dust he laboured as hard and as long as the people whose life depended upon it.

Watching him from a distance, eyes wide with wonder, was the mustard grower's apprentice, Hiawatha Longfellow. When he looked at Dylan, he saw the promise of an outside world of exciting possibilities and perhaps his own bright future.

On the southern stretch of Bet Road, where it bridges the now dry bed of the Henry, there stands the public house and garden. The garden is on the river bank, although it is hardly what may be described as ornamental, it did offer a grand view of the river and the boundary trees that marked the border of the arable farmland managed by William Absurd on the south bank.

On warm summer evenings, when the villagers met at the pub, the garden was busy with the reclining workers relaxing socially and enjoying the sight and sound of the beloved Henry with its complement of ducks and moorfowl. This particular evening saw the locals gathered as usual at the pub garden. The circumstances were very different though, as they worried and speculated about the state of crisis into which they had been plunged.

Dylan sat and listened until he began to understand what was going on. A cup of Mustik had been placed in his hand by Athena when he had first arrived, though he had been so absorbed in the conversation it had rested forgotten in his hand. Uther Smith made his way to Dylan's side to thank him for his contribution to the day's work.

"How are ye friend Dylan?" he asked with one hand on the other man's shoulder to assist his descent, as he manoeuvred himself wearily into a sitting position on the grass. Dylan raised one hand to the bandage, reminded at last about the cause of his headache he responded positively, saying "Much better thanks". Uther smiled and squeezed the younger man's shoulder as an expression of his empathy.

"Thank ye for your work today. Ye certainly bent your

back to it and we needed every pair of hands we could get"

"The woman who helped me..." Dylan began

"Miss Pippin." said Uther, by way of belated introduction.

"Miss Pippin," confirmed Dylan "Is she going to be alright?" Uther's face broke into an open smile and then he laughed briefly.

"She will be fine, lad. Aye, I'm sure she will be fine. Thank ye for your concern." Uther raised his mug of mead "Ye need a bed and a meal I am certain, will ye give me the pleasure of giving ye food and rest while ye stay"

Dylan was surprised and pleased at the offer and accepted without hesitation. This seemed to be to Uther's liking, as he raised his mug again and took a deep gulp of mead: Dylan, suddenly aware that he too had a mug of liquid, raised it to his lips and took a swallow. Everyone in the garden cheered as Dylan shot to his feet with his eyes watering and gasping in shock at the sheer viciousness of the Mustik he had just imbibed. It seemed to him to be a small demon with many teeth and claws with which to resist going down the throat. The raw feeling it left him with made him cough heartily, as every villager rejoiced, as was their tradition, at the initiation of another Mustik drinker to their curiously infertile ranks.

Chapter Eight

Frightened, hurt, and scratched still more as he progressed, Dean Baxter ran on without noting his direction, hoping that he would eventually stumble upon the road less travelled by which he had arrived. He had little grasp of the scale of the valley and his stumbling had been all in the wrong direction. Now without shelter, without the weapon, without the stolen money and without dignity, he finally gave into exhaustion and collapsed. Hugging his bloody knees up to his heaving chest he put his mud streaked face down and sobbed quietly until sleep claimed him.

A rough blanket was pulled over his shoulders as he slept, and his exhaustion was such that even when a fire pit was dug beside him, stocked with firewood and lit, it didn't penetrate his spent consciousness that drifted elsewhere to protect him from the pain that wracked his skinny frame.

The sun was making good progress across a blue sky when Baxter awoke. That first glimpse of warmth almost elicited a smile before the rancid taste of recent events soured the flavour of the day and brought him back to his miserable self. With every intention of burrowing back into the oneiric respite of hibernation standard unconsciousness, he was suddenly aware of a rough cloth against his hand. He sat up sharply and gasped at the sight of the blanket and then again at the implications of the covering.

In his second glance he took in the fire pit with stones about it to contain the glowing embers and on the top of a stone with a flatter surface was a bread roll.

Baxter looked about him for the signs of a trap or to wake from the dream, but no such sign was forthcoming. He paused to listen but nothing that reached his ears was anything to him.

Seizing the bun, he bit into the solid crust sending a shower of crisp crumbs about him, chewing appreciatively on the bread while peering into a cup that stood nearby away from the fire, and noting that it contained water. It was at that moment that he realised how hungry and thirsty he was. Having enjoyed a cursory chew of the first mouthful of bread, he took a second bite as he discovered that he was so parched that he could not swallow the first.

The water was enough to ease the passage of the food, and as he progressed through the breakfast he was thinking that it was such a small amount of food, but when he had finished it he realised that it had more body and substance than the bread he had eaten in the past. Not full, but by no means still hungry, he wrapped the blanket about himself and stood up, seeking sign or token of his benefactor, feeling a small unaccustomed glow of gratitude to the unseen Samaritan but still fearful of the motive.

As he stood wondering a figure loomed suddenly and silently out of the bushes and stooping for the cup, indicated with a wave that Baxter should follow him.

"Who...?" began Baxter, but was cut off by the figure turning and standing nose to nose with him, simply voiced a low "Shhhhhhh!" and in a conspiratorial manner moved between the bushes without noise. Baxter took a brief look about himself before following the path taken by the odd man, who looked back once with a look of exasperation at the crunching of twigs and leaves beneath Baxter's feet as he advertised his blundering progress.

Chapter Nine

Ballentine Trimble looked with unashamed admiration at the tired and grubby form of Mavis Stranger as she wearily sought his face among the gathered workers. With the zeal of a woman reborn in the world with a purpose and awarded respect she thought would never be hers again, she had worked alongside the villagers, shared bread and laughter with them in this time of great uncertainty, and now she was looking for the comfort of Ballentine's sedate company to round off a perfect day.

Clae had claimed Mavis, and subverted all those dreary thoughts of purposeless dotage and pushed them aside with thoughts of community and the grime and exhaustion that quells aimless wanderlust and satisfies the muscles and spirit after a day of honest toil alongside careful people.

Bally raised a hand in signal and invitation, to which she responded by blushing like an adolescent and sitting beside him on the grass. Mavis had been acutely conscious of the years leaving signs of their passage on her features as she noticed that she drew fewer glances from people until at last she realised with a strong cocktail mixed with equal jiggers of relief and regret, she had evaporated like alcohol, faded from view, an invisible woman of a certain age. All of those concerns that had preoccupied her as a young woman were less of a concern as she dressed to please herself and to suit the weather, rather than to pass the judgement of men and the even less forgiving scrutiny of other women. Yet within her, the heart and mind remained the youthful twenty three years of age that she would offer as her age if somebody, catching her unawares, should ask of her. That immediate response was still on her lips when she would, with a growing sense of alarm, revise that number up in stages until the true account was told by the depth of the furrow on her brow as she rushed headlong through a montage of scenes recaptured from a long and largely happy life, to arrive at the same unwelcome, sneering, betrayal she had come to accept from mirrors. Mavis was now the willing captive of a society in which she had a place, a use, a value and above all else, she had a presence; no longer invisible, because every age of human development, from babe to elder, had a role in this backwoods community. This was something that Mavis could not easily relinquish even after so short a time as she had known it, the hilltop had been her Rubicon,

    Ballentine regretted that there was not sufficient water available to heat up a bath for her, in which she could relax and sip at a glass of Bramble wine from his personal cellar boasting wine of past years including the glorious 1979. It had been a terrible year for wheat, but the blackberries had grown in such numbers they were hard pressed to collect them in. Last year had been good for apples and they had been hard pressed into cider.

"What became of the newcomers?" she asked of Bally. He was pouring her a cup of clear water and nodded in the direction of Uther and Dylan.

"I think it is a good job we don't get too many visitors" he noted as Mavis accepted the cup and sipped appreciatively.

"The local council did consider buying this land from the Ministry of Defence at one point, many years ago" She recalled in conversational tones "…but they decided the hills were too riddled with ancient mines, caves and littered with unexploded ordnance to be worth the effort and the Ministry of Defence were not keen on the idea either. Too many mines of one sort or another"

Bally laughed and whispered to her that "Even the sheep don't bother trying to get over them hills"

Mavis asked after Desdemona Pippin and Uther responded to her enquiry.

"Miss Pippin thinks it unhealthsome to be pointing guns at folk in the public convenience. It's right inconvenient if she wants to put some cut flowers in there. So she goes in anyway."

"Goodness" exclaimed Mavis with concern "The danger! Somebody could have been seriously hurt."

"That's true" agreed Uther "But I don't think she did him any permanent damage". His laughter at his own joke was echoed by those within earshot who all knew the truth of what he said and were all, by now, aware that their beloved matriarch was recovering well.

"Where is the young man with the gun?" asked Mavis. Quizzical glances were exchanged and Uther finally had to admit that he had run off.

"What if he should come back?" asked Mavis with concern. Uther was unconcerned about the prospect; "Why should he come back here, to a village with no river?" The crowd fell silent as they again contemplated life without The River Henry to feed it.

Dylan shuddered at the prospect of Baxter returning to the village, then he shuddered again at the prospect of Baxter returning to the town with stories of Clae and how quickly the village would fall prey to the voracious new world outside, and this last enclave of humanity would be mopped up like a stain.

Uther Smith lives in a small cottage near the brewery, afforded more space than some by the fact that he lived alone.

Not a lonely existence by any means, but his position as a community leader made him less approachable to some, though his gregarious nature was sometimes at odds with long evenings alone during the dark days of winter. The extra space he was afforded allowed some considerable industry on his part in the making and storing of preserves. Such was his skill that young children would collect his fruit for him to be rewarded with a jar of preserve to take home like a trophy to an appreciative household. Due to this extracurricular activity his home was largely given over to the production and storage of preserves and a few assorted wines and beverages with which he liked to experiment as an extension of his life as a brewer. Athena Slough would often assist in this as she learnt the trade and sought to understand the various facets of the process.

As Dylan was eagerly ushered into the dark cottage by an enthusiastic Uther, he was struck by the collection of utensils that were used in making the preserves. Admittedly they were hanging from a beam just inside the door and it was dark, but Dylan made his way straight into them and made them clatter like a diesel engine starting on a cold morning.

Uther apologised and guided him unerringly to an overstuffed armchair by the fireplace, at which point Uther found, and lit a candle by virtue of long practice and touch. When the glow lit the room and Dylan was able to appreciate what a cluttered place it was from the vantage point of what was obviously Uther's favourite chair, sharing some his characteristics as it did, being as soft and wide as Uther himself.

Dylan could but wonder at the collection of items stored and displayed around the place. Instead of books, there were shelves lined with jars of preserves, the jars themselves varied from stoneware pots with wooden stoppers to heavy glass jars that appeared to have been made in Victorian times. Each was carefully marked with a small wooden label tied on to the rim of the jar with a woven grass string. The same string could be seen in various stages of production, half woven, drying, or finished and wound into small loops and tied around the middle, the wasp waist products of long evenings alone in the fading light.

Elsewhere candles could be seen, either waiting to be used, two looped by their shared wick over a nail in the beam or waiting to be dipped in tallow again. There was a small hand loom in a corner with some rough cloth in production, and a few pictures on the walls in various styles, depicting people or places from the village. The older the picture, the more haze had accumulated from the candles and fires that had coated them with smuts and a distinctive greasy sheen.

Dylan looked about him in wonder, as he wondered what some of the items were and who the portraits depicted and wondered where he would sleep. Uther meanwhile stood in excited anticipation of some comment on the luxurious nature of his domicile. Dylan awoke suddenly to his hosts need and exclaimed at his surroundings "What a lovely place you have here. I would be interested to know about some of the things I see around the room". Uther fairly expanded with pleasure at the praise and gleefully assured Dylan "In the morning I will show ye the rest of the house."

With a small fire in the grate and each with a cup of mead, Uther extinguished the candle to let the firelight provide the illumination and save the precious resource for another occasion. The subdued light took away the need to make eye contact which relieved Dylan of the unfamiliar experience of thinking he was making eye contact when in fact it just happened to be the direction in which Uther's lazy eye had chosen to rest. Eye contact was now impossible as the deepening dark cast both men into the privacy of shadow. Dylan's trauma and his busy day gradually crept upon him and lulled him to sleep as Uther happily related the history of the village in anecdotes and tales. When he noticed that his guest had dropped off Uther smiled and relieved him of the drink cradled in cupped hands on his lap, he fetched a sturdy blanket and covered the young man, and left him to sleep, as he retreated to his bed.

What dreams visited Dylan that night and what fancies overtook him when he considered the world in which he found himself and his unconscious mind unravelled his experiences and his rational side told him it was just wish fulfilment. When the light of dawn crept through the branches of the plum tree outside Uther's cottage and flickered across Dylan's face to gently wake him, he was disoriented as if he had woken from a dream to find he had not woken at all and the dream continued. Only this time the world he had known faded and the dream of Clae asserted itself as the dominant reality, and what was that delicious smell?

That unidentified aroma was an omelette containing various plants that the outside world would dismiss as weeds. Peppery dandelion leaves wild garlic and herbs, along with some roots that were known to the villagers gave a delicious flavour to the fresh eggs collected that morning from one of the henhouses that were dotted about the village. The omelette was fried in a heavy skillet, one of the valuable metal utensils that either predated the isolationist period of the region or were made by the smith from the ore dug from the surrounding hills, in a method passed from smith to apprentice for generations. No metal object was discarded in this parish, but submitted to the Smith for repair or for melting down.

As fresh fire danced in the grate to keep away the morning chill, Dylan doubted if the breakfast would have tasted so wonderful had he not been far hungrier than he realised, but at every mouthful he relished the new tastes that insinuated themselves upon his palate. Uther was again delighted by the genuine compliment the young man's appetite bestowed upon his culinary skills. But neither had cleared their plate before a blushing Athena Slough arrived at the door to greet Uther but looking past him to meet Dylan's eyes as he paused with wooden fork poised between plate and open mouth, transfixed by the sight of the young woman, dark hair cascading about her shoulders and eyes shining, now laughing at Dylan's comical pose and bringing him to himself, at which he was almost disposed to forget his meal, but good sense won out, and the waiting forkful was despatched with eyes open that he could enjoy both the flavour of the food and the sight of Athena smiling.

Uther was momentarily discombobulated, as he was not sure if he should encourage or forbid such a relationship between Dylan and Athena. Inevitably he decided to defer to Desdemona's opinion as she always knew what was best when it came to those problems that Uther could not understand. It was an excuse to visit with her too, and his concern was genuine even if he failed to recognise the depth of his affection for the indomitable Miss Pippin. Had he given it any further thought, he would have realised that Athena should make up her own mind, after all she was the chosen heir to Desdemona's position, but Uther was just too content with an excuse to visit with her so he guided Athena out of the doorway towards the brewery in case the young folk should resolve the issue alone and deprive him of his pretext.

 Putting aside his offer to show Dylan the rest of his cottage, Uther suggested Dylan explore the village and its environs while Athena and he went to the distillery to see what could be done there. Dylan reluctantly stepped outside holding his eye contact with Athena to the last moment while she smiled encouragement until he was lost to her sight. Uther then busied himself with some minor chores while Athena stocked a pot with an assortment of herbs and vegetables and set it over the fire before she and Uther set off for their place of work.

 Dylan decided to look around and find out more about the village and how he could make himself useful. He walked alongside the dry riverbed to the millpond and helped the people there erecting a frame for a shaduf with which water could be fetched from the pond without risk of slipping mud into the water, or frightening the ducks, which was the concern of Shylock Giza who loved his ducks and the eggs which made his pastries so light. Villagers introduced themselves and slapped him on the back as he pitched in and made himself welcome.

When the frame and boom were lashed together and the mechanism tested, Dylan walked on to discover fields of sugar beet. Small cottages and cabins were dotted about and each person he encountered seemed to be contentedly busy at some vital task, but not so busy that they couldn't stop and ask him endless questions about his part in the drama or about the world outside. He answered as honestly as he was able but he felt that the questions were aimed at something his answers apparently failed to provide. After a number of such encounters he realised that it was him they were interested and the questions were designed to give the stranger a context rather than to find out about his world.

Eventually he found himself in an orchard where chickens, geese and sheep roamed among the trees. He found a cabin hidden among the trees, almost indistinguishable from the woodland as the growing hazel seemed to form part of the walls; the thatch and turf roof was part structure and part growth. Outside the cabin on a stump sat a slender weathered man, his leathery hands busy with wooden frames that he was making with some care and more than a little skill. He apparently knew Dylan was there but paid no attention to him. Dylan watched for a while and was about to leave when the man looked up from his work and fixed the visitor with a look that caused Dylan to remember the Rime of the Ancient Mariner, as he was held by the glittering eye of the older man.

Yet there was no tale of mystical woe but an appraisal and a challenge. Dylan considered speaking, even opening his mouth at one point, but detecting an almost imperceptible shift in the other man's countenance he held his tongue and continued to stand in silence until the other fellow seemed to be satisfied and nodded once before carrying on with his work and paying no more attention to Dylan than he did to a bee that buzzed about his head as he worked, not even bothering to wave a hand at these distractions.

Thus, summarily released, Dylan paused only a moment before continuing on his way, puzzled by the encounter and yet feeling that he had somehow passed the test, which in fact he had, as the beekeeper making his frames was not easy company and had few friends; he loathed idle chatter, being a champion of silence and a practitioner of the same. It was the inability of folk to keep their peace that irritated him, and the stranger had not felt the need to fill that sacred void with foolish questions or needless introductions, but the looks they had exchanged told him all he wanted to know; that he liked the lad, and the lad had shown respect for his custom. Perhaps next time they met he may exchange a greeting, possibly even a verbal one.

As Dylan bimbled along he noted that there seemed to be no patch of land not utilised in growing something useful to the village, be it a food crop or trees, reeds for thatch or woven mats and rush lights, grass for hay. Even the turned down corners of gardens or the dog eared edges of the few lawns were places reserved for some herb to flourish and eventually be turned to culinary or medicinal purposes.

Every cell in his body was beginning to drop into phase with the village. The armour he had constructed for himself was useless to him here as he no longer required it to deflect the society that valued the sounds of activity. He cherished the comfortable caress of silence, or what passed for silence in the sibilant trees, the glottal raindrops, the labial murmur of the river, the voiced plosives of thunder or the fricative birdsong: all of it together was the language of the planet as it breathed the meaning of life, spelling out the year in four acts, each with subtlety and hints at the other phases of other moons.

He had lost the taste for noise in the form of machinery's grinding, music's ululations, conversation's rattle, or the pervasive, perverse, vinegary whine of the media.

His armour seemed to dog his every move. He felt cumbersome and awkward but unable to shed the burden on demand. The fear he had fostered, threatened unimagined horror on the heart without a stout shield. Yet, here he was despairing at the very idea of ever leaving this place where life was in every breath, and not saved up for weekends and holidays, or put on hold for some glint on the horizon. He had always felt that time was like a tidal bore roaring destructively towards a catastrophe, but here he felt that time passing was the gentle flow of a stream making its way to a balmy ocean, a journey he was delighted to contemplate.

Athena saw in Dylan the promise of a kindred outlook, a person who would be pleased to walk beside her, in step, without competition for supremacy. An outsider, with knowledge of a wider world and all of its wonders, how could such a person settle for the life that she loved? The outside did not frighten her, but had no appeal as she was defined by her context, as a part of the organism of Clae.

Like Canute she hopelessly ordered the tide to turn and take her thoughts of what would never be, away from her. Musings threatening to caress her with warm and peaceful all embracing hope. A whisper of what she dared not dream for fear of the pain it would cause if she was correct in her guess: she calculated that without deep roots such as her own, he would blow away on the next breeze to cross the hills.

The instant attraction she had experienced was probably a mistake, she decided, and it would pass, as he would pass, and life would return to normal, but what of this pain? People spoke of the heart, but her stomach hurt as if her longing was almost a hunger and again she had to master her imaginings, push away the unbidden wondering about a wanderer.

Chapter Ten

Collitt Semper had cause to regret the tall tales he had spun to entertain his young apprentice, as he had planted the seed of adventure in the mind of Hiawatha Longfellow, and the vine that grew was cluttering his mind with expansive dreams of what lay beyond. His explorer's soul yearned to see behind the bounding line of the tantalising horizon and travel to the exotic places that he had seen in Ballentine's books. He longed to be Robinson Crusoe and see that footprint on the tropical shore, or Walter Raleigh discovering new lands, only partially cognisant of the fact that those lands had long ago been discovered by those who were living there when the Europeans first arrived to claim those inhabited places as their own.

     Still the unknown world around beckoned him in his dreams, and Dylan with his strange clothes and speech seemed to be representative of the wider world and not threatening, or dangerous. Baxter was not part of the equation as he was an uncomfortable fit in this syllogism. Mavis of course had been running away from that world but was already part of the community so the thought of asking her was still at the periphery of his thoughts, pressing the button and waiting for the lights to change before crossing his mind.

By the shores of River Henry,
By the shining Mill-Pond-Water,
Stood the Home of Shylock Giza,
Companion of the Moon, Was Giza.
Dark behind it rose the hilltops,
Thick with thorns and gloomy pine-trees,

Rose the hills with firs upon them;
Bright before it beat the water,
Beat the clear and sunny water,
Beat the shining Mill-Pond-Water.
There the wrinkled Shylock Giza
Taught the little Hiawatha,
When he left his linden cradle,
Bedded soft in moss and rushes.
Many things Old Shylock taught him
Of the things beyond the valley.

    How could he leave poor Collitt without a prentice to help him? Collitt had been so kind to him extending his warmth to young Hiawatha and treating him with respect and consideration. His parents too and his friends would all suffer the loss of him should he go. Should he go?

    Dylan could advise him and that would be something on which to base an informed decision. His mind was made up to speak with Dylan.

    The whole village knew that Dylan was the guest of Uther Smith, so it was Uther's door that Hiawatha opened to see if he could locate the elusive newcomer, but an empty silent cottage met his enquiry though two strange bundles sat beside the front door, both were contained in smooth glossy material he had never seen and one was of a strange shape while the other was a mess of straps and tiny metal teeth. His curiosity was short lived as the urgency of his mission asserted its authority, and he abandoned the empty cottage and empty speculation in search of Dylan or Uther.

From outside Uther's house he looked about himself and glimpsed in the north, a figure walking through Collitt Semper's mustard fields from the orchards to the west of the village. He could tell it was Dylan who was heading towards him, so he sat down to await the other's arrival.

Dylan was too cocooned in the stifling isolation of a reverie as heavy and warm as a duvet, to have any sense of what may be outside, so he was almost upon Hiawatha Longfellow before he noticed him.

"Good day" said Hiawatha climbing to his feet, startling Dylan back into the present.

Dylan was a little off balance but stumbled through a greeting of sorts with a garble "Ah yes… good aft… Morn… Hello, to see you…" Hiawatha smiled at the strange salutation but said no more until Dylan had looked about him, presumably to locate and collect his thoughts. When sufficient time had passed to allow his retrieval of even the most fleeting of ideas before it escaped entirely, Dylan once again faced Hiawatha to meet his gaze and make a proper greeting.

"How are you?" he asked in the time honoured phatic style of the world, but Hiawatha was raised to different standards and mistook the social overture for a whole movement; so it was with a slightly puzzled frown he assured Dylan that he had not been unwell, before inviting Dylan to sit with him while he made his own slow approach to the questions he had to ask.

Dylan was used to a few exchanges of rhetorical questions and pat answers in the way whole exchanges on the topic of the weather can be negotiated by strangers, whilst the whole time maintaining a comfortable distance from any form of real communication. The slow purposeful approach to conversation which aimed at an exchange of ideas was something new to him, but he identified the form and purpose of the style and learned quickly the rudiments of its etiquette.

Hiawatha asked Dylan about himself and told his own story, each paying more attention to the answers as they revealed more of the character of each until Hiawatha had reached the point where he felt he knew enough of Dylan to be able to ask him the serious questions. The conversational overture had been leisurely and long but now that Hiawatha was rosined and tuned, the pizzicato questions were allegrissimo.

Dylan found the early questions easy to answer: "Why are ye called Dylan?" asked Hiawatha expecting some revealing tale about the choice. "It's not my name really. It's a nickname given to me because I play the guitar and sing". The confusion evident in the harrowed lines on Hiawatha's forehead prompted further explanation. "There is a famous singer who has the same first name as me, so my friends called me Dylan as a joke, but after a while it became my name, in a way."

"What is your name?"

"Robert"

"What should I call ye?"

"Dylan"

"Why? If it is not your name…"

"It is what my friends call me"

The look with which Hiawatha responded to that last comment made Dylan feel humble before the gratitude of a person who made no disposable remarks about friendship.

Then came an awkward turn in the conversation, which was to test the new friendship to it limits.

"What is it like outside the village?" asked Hiawatha, poised attentively with large eyes.

Dylan felt a wave of nausea as he briefly considered the thought of the citizens of Clae adrift in the world he knew, or worse still the insanely predatory world coming here to a defenceless oasis of sanity.

Lying did not come easily to Dylan, so he discarded the possibility of creating horror stories of the life he had known, though selected episodes would have made a frightening enough tale to tell as a deterrent. The thought of encouraging the wanderlust apparent in the question was also abhorrent as it would make him complicit if Hiawatha was to abscond.

"One thing I must tell you before I say anything else" Dylan warned with all the gravity he could muster, "Clae would be destroyed if anybody outside the village got to know of its existence."

Hiawatha nodded with due solemnity, but Dylan was not in the market for trite gestures.

"Tell me you understand and believe me before I say another word" continued Dylan in the same tone.

Hiawatha looked at him with a little fear apparent in his eyes and paused briefly before making reply.

"I understand ye, and if I should ever go outside the village, I shall keep Clae hidden if ye think it will protect us all"

Though far from satisfied, Dylan was at least assured

that the young man understood the serious implications he believed would be the consequence of revealing the village to the wider world.

Holding Hiawatha's gaze for a moment longer than either found entirely comfortable to further illustrate the serious nature of his message, Dylan at last enquired of him what it was he wished to hear.

"What has been discovered since the war?" was the first question to come at Dylan with such blunt force that he was unable to neatly sidestep like a matador with blinding flicker of red silken sophistry, but struck dumb by the ambiguity and enormity of the query.

"Which war?" He countered, with some relief that he had a moment to regain his balance.

"The third big one when we were bombed again" explained Hiawatha, somewhat confused that it had not been obvious.

Unfortunately, Dylan was at a loss, as he had no knowledge of the Ministry allowing the army to shell the hills and the way that had been interpreted by the fearful residents. He decided to go with the Second World War and begin there, but then he realised that he had no idea where to begin.

It seemed reasonable that he should start with the major

differences that he had experienced. So he began by trying to explain Television. Before long a small crowd had gathered about and were listening intently to the tortuous description of the single biggest revolution in entertainment since the wireless. Having stumbled through an explanation that he feared did no justice to the iconic equipment that was the focus of most sitting rooms across the land, if not the world, he moved on to attempt descriptions of cars, computers, mobile phones and finally as the sun dipped below the hills he tried in vain to explain how almost all remote corners of the world had now been explored and mapped, with the exception of the deepest regions of the ocean floors and perhaps Clae, although that last part was something that caused him to wonder a little.

    By the time Uther had finished meeting with the other senior figures in the village hierarchy, discussing plans and policies for dealing with the crisis, Dylan had talked himself hoarse and answered so many questions he had lapsed his intention of guarding his responses and had been as open as usual, eliciting some gasps of astonishment and incredulity from the audience; he was very glad to be pulled away from the group by Uther promising food and rest from the questions.

Clae

Chapter Eleven

Before Uther had set off with Athena that morning he had been lulled into a temporary state of contentment, as the man who was having the privilege of entertaining one of the two visitors to the village, an event unprecedented in his memory, an occasion, an entertainment and something about which he could claim some reflected glory, the channel through which others may seek an audience with the newcomer or a route by which they could seek information. It was his position and pleasure to gain as much news and intelligence of the modern world from his guest as possible.

Of course the whole situation was but a respite from the horror of the current crisis, but the enormity of the problem, the loss of their water source, was so great that it refused to remain as a reality in his consciousness, allowing his attentions to slip aside from direct confrontation of the situation.

However, once Athena had dragged him away, and he walked to the brewery and saw the sluices dry, his mouth quickly became equally arid, his voice thickened with dark emotional overtones as he directed the workers to bottling water rather than brewing Mustik. Ben Caliban was busy adapting the plant to its new purpose without need of being told, Athena was also quick to adapt to the situation and also to assist with the tasks at hand.

Uther could not get out of the brewery quickly enough, his position of authority uppermost in his mind as his treacherous body seemed determined to waste water through tears as his friends and colleagues sought to preserve it, and he was conscious that he must at least give the impression of confidence in the certainty of salvation.

The manor house was the meeting place for some of the village elders coming together to discuss and plan for the future of the village in the face of a foe that was as formidable as any they had ever met.

Uther called the meeting to order as the delegates chatted urgently but informally amongst themselves. Reluctantly the smaller conversations faded and all focussed upon Uther.

"We have some water for drinking and a little for irrigation at the millpond, but we have only about a week before the crops suffer for it"

Daisy Thruppence, and her husband Nebuchadnezzar were in attendance. Daisy could always be relied upon to speak but it was Nebuchadnezzar who spoke after careful consideration; it was often the case that folk had no choice but to listen to Daisy but when Nebuchadnezzar spoke they would willingly attend to his words.

This couple were workers on the vegetable fields of the land managed by William Absurd. Their involvement in civic affairs was largely on the strength of their interest, their kindness and the mental acuity of Nebuchadnezzar.

Shylock Giza was uncharacteristically solemn, as he sat with his hands on the large dining table contemplating his fingers while the group settled. William Absurd and Ophelia Luckett were there, side by side but without the energy or spirit for the usual cut and thrust of their symbolic sparring.

Collitt Semper regarded the group with Frank Curiosity, inseparable as ever, but not as jocular as they had been at the marketplace. Their usual disposition having been subdued by the first real emergency to test the group, and each now doubting if they were the right person to occupy the chair in which they sat, representative of the figures in which the villagers had placed their trust and their hope.

Ophelia Luckett cleared her throat tentatively and all eyes focussed on her in desperate optimism. Blushing in the spotlight of attentive, misplaced faith that her words would provide the answer they so needed, she cleared her throat again and looked down before she muttered "The land around Pinnock's Paddock is flooded and I have tried to use the water to irrigate the fields nearest the paddock, but if we could drain the paddock it could provide some water."

A flatulent grumble of agreement wafted around the room, wrinkling noses in disappointment before it dispersed.

"I shall ask Ben Caliban to find a way to do that" said Uther, looking hopefully about him to see if any further contributions could sprinkle some spice of positivity into the thin cloudy broth of their fast rations of humour.

Even Daisy Thruppence had no stomach for idle chatter, so it was with enormous relief that Nebuchadnezzar's voice broke the leaden silence.

"Whatever ails The Henry River is outside the village and there are two among us who know about that world and could seek out both cause and solution."

"Well I know of one that won't be going there" said a familiar voice from the doorway. All eyes swivelled immediately to the stately Desdemona Pippin arriving to take her place at the table, and as the others were overcoming their disbelief at her presence, Uther was on his feet and embracing her with joy.

"Get off ye great fool" she told him gently "I'm like to be smothered by ye"

Uther pulled out a chair for her and regained his own, while all the delegates studiously ignored the tears of joy in his eyes and more than a few blinked rapidly for a few moments as if Desdemona was too bright for such a dingy atmosphere.

Without pausing for well wishing and questions, she continued with her thoughts on the subject of the newcomers.

"Mavis is in no condition to make such a journey, and Ballentine would be quick to object. We shouldn't even think on that unless there's folk to go with her, but Nebuchadnezzar has the right of it as ever."

Nebuchadnezzar showed no hint of satisfaction in this praise, and the assembly nodded agreement as they considered what they could ask of Dylan.

"Why would he do it?" asked Daisy with a sidelong glance at her husband that suggested that although Nebuchadnezzar may be a man of few words, they were seldom the last.

"Why would he refuse?" countered Uther with his customary smile making a cautious but welcome return. Frank took up the cause with enthusiasm "True he worked long and hard with us when we needed him yesterday, I've no reason to think he would refuse us."

"If not him, then one of us will go" said Nebuchadnezzar, stating what none had really considered. While each inwardly considered the bleak possibility of venturing out of the place of their birth, Desdemona broke their reverie.

"We had best ask the lad then. Tonight"

Somewhat fortified by the chance to take some action, the group rallied to discuss other related issues and decide how best to prepare for the days ahead.

By the time the table was vacated, and Desdemona could fend off no more questions about her health and details of her encounter with Dean Baxter, the sun was dipping towards the hills and Uther took it upon himself to feed Dylan and then deliver him to the garden of the Pub on the banks of the dry bed where, until very recently The Henry had flowed. The pub, which was known as 'The Pub' had a bar and garden which was the traditional evening meeting place for many of the villagers, but tonight Uther felt that it was a terrible destination, and a Christian may draw parallels with the garden of Gethsemane, where he was to deliver young Dylan up to what Uther would consider a fate far worse than death. Though he reasoned it would not hold the same dread for Dylan he still felt it was a betrayal of trust and a crime against hospitality to lead him there without telling what was planned, or at least to prepare him in some way: so it was with a forced jollity that he greeted Dylan sitting on the ground holding court with a group of villagers that evening.

Dylan was ready for a meal though distracted sufficiently for the fact to have escaped his notice, but when Uther's heavy hand and tight smile eased him away from his audience to their collective dismay; the promise of food was sufficient enticement. Uther guided him away to his home where they noticed the bags on the doorstep straight away. The packages that had piqued Hiawatha's curiosity were similarly bewildering to Uther, though Dylan immediately recognised both and whooped with joy at their arrival.

"My guitar and my pack!" he exclaimed "How did they get here?" He turned to Uther with a smile and words of gratitude about to burst forth but Uther's bewildered innocence converted the words into a small undignified squeak of confused excitement at the reunion of traveller and lost belongings.

As Dylan heaved the pack and guitar case indoors Uther set about serving up two bowls of steaming stew that had been slow cooking all day in the embers of that morning's fire, that hunger had bobbed to the surface of his consciousness and was now pin sharp and demanding.

The pair ate in silence, Dylan assuming this was the companionable norm and Uther feeling that every second was a tacit condemnation of his duplicity and dishonour until he could stand it no longer and decided to speak his turbulent mind.

"The elders met and have decided to ask ye to help" he blurted. Dylan paused with his mouth open and the spoon midway between bowl and lip; hunger versus curiosity; which appetite should he satisfy first? The spoon retuned slowly to the bowl and his mouth closed as he cocked an inquiring eyebrow at Uther.

In his turn the older man revealed the gist of the meeting and the position into which he was placed and his misgivings about it. The whole time he regarded Dylan with questioning gaze for sign or token of condemnation or a chance of redemption.

At first Dylan was alarmed at the prospect of returning so soon to the world outside, but he saw the logic of the decision made by the Elders, and that decision had been to ask him, not command him, to help them set the situation right. He saw no mischief or animosity in the request, but he also sensed the substance and cause of Uther's discomfiture. Uther finished his explanation and still saw no clear sign of a reaction in Dylan's face, but fell silent, awaiting judgement.

"It makes sense for me to go I suppose, though I shall miss this place and the people I have met"

"Then come back to us" replied Uther, with a broad smile

of gratitude and relief. Now they could enjoy the meal and approached The Pub with something that looked like good spirits, at least from a distance.

Dylan's mind was reeling with the sudden influx of philosophical questions and existential angst, as he struggled to pull together all the loose threads of the situation and plait them into a tight bell rope that could ring the changes, and allow opportunity to chime rather than any feeble knocking. It was difficult to hold onto those threads as they were diverse and sometimes mutually opposed, so he worried about the fate of Clae if the outside world was to hear of it: he worried about the fate of Clae if the outside world did nothing about the dry river. Was it necessary to reveal the existence of Clae to rescue it's water supply?

He knew that his personal interest in the village was the reason all of these concerns seemed so immediate and pressing in upon him and yet more strands presented themselves as he considered Athena, to whom he was attracted more than anybody he had ever met: Athena who was a creature of Clae, and who may not flourish in a modern world. Indeed it was apparent to him that the people of the village were ill equipped to deal with the concerns of modern life. What did they care for ambition, acquisition, wealth or luxury? This context made the whole focus of life the community while the developed world was fuelled by drives and motivations alien to this microcosm. They could be given the contents of a bank vault and it would mean nothing to them.

If Dean Baxter had left that money behind they would have puzzled over it and ultimately forgotten it, but thinking about the bank robber made him realise that he had pushed back thoughts of the armed robber until now. He realised with horror that a desperado with no weapon, no money and no food would have to head back to the civilisation he knew, and he would have a story to tell. As quickly as the thought asserted itself he realised that the story was one whose secrecy, self preservation should protect; if the miscreant breathed a word of the village and his journey there, the folk who lived here would have their own story to tell and it was one that would guarantee him a lengthy term of penal servitude.

The thought was now unravelled and the remaining threads no less elusive, but Dylan was busy putting aside his own desires and wishes to concentrate on what he must do for the village and what he could offer. It was possible that Athena would not think more of him for his willingness to help, but he was sure that she would think less of him if he refused. It was Athena as much as the rest of the village that he was keen to preserve, so he persuaded himself to take the honourable course and if possible to enjoy it.

It was time for Dylan to look through his pack and wonder who had left it at Uther's door. Uther hid his wonder at the zips as he thought it polite to show no naked curiosity at the things belonging to the stranger. Dylan, concentrating on his rucksack, found everything in its place from the items of clothing rolled up and stuffed around the wood burning camping stove and nest of pans. A folding trowel, first aid kit, a lock knife with four inch blade, a small shaving mirror and safety razor, a towel, canvas rubber soled shoes, toilet roll, a wind-up torch and some dried foods along with a small sewing kit, sail maker's palm needles and whipping twine for tent and clothing repairs, a water bottle with a built in filter with a spare filter, a high quality camping knife with multiple blades and a small one man tent, sleeping bag and cotton sleeping bag liner.

The other case contained his acoustic guitar, a plectrum, some loose sheets of music, some hand written, spare guitar strings, pitch pipes and a few paperback books which made Uther's eyes light up at the prospect of new reading matter, not on his own account, but on behalf of the village readers who would fall upon new reading material with an alacrity bordering on the vulgar. Of course the pleasure that Uther anticipated was the casual dissemination of the news that there were new books in the village. It had not even occurred to him that Dylan might withhold the books as the library was all that the village folk knew of such items and those volumes were communal property.

The guitar had also caused Uther to sit up straighter and look on with ill concealed anticipation, and an equal measure of disappointment when Dylan shut the case and pulled the straps closed. Uther had to clear his throat twice before suggesting as casually as he was able, that Dylan should bring his guitar with him to The Pub. In response, Dylan laughed off the suggestion, but Uther leaned forward, clasped the younger man by the wrist and making eye contact he said "A tune or two would be well received if ye could bring yourself to play for us at the pub".

With a sudden insight, Dylan appreciated the importance of entertainment and realised why some unseen hand had left the guitar on the doorstep of Uther's cottage. Without wireless or Television, without cinema or gramophone, the entertainment was produced by the people with any aptitude. Even though he sensed a certain immunity from criticism implied by Uther's intensity of longing, it was with a thrill of nervous energy that he reluctantly agreed to the request.

Clae

Chapter Twelve

It was late, and dark, before Uther made any sign of heading out of doors. At long last he proposed a walk.

The darkness seemed heavy and thick to Dylan, accustomed to streets lit around him overtly lighting the avenues or the same insinuated by the orange glow that lights the skies near any conurbation of sufficient size. Only occasionally had he seen darkness as complete as this one that settled about Clae as water surrounds a diver; a blackstrap molasses variety of night, with only the pinpricks of candlelight at cottage windows to betray any life or activity about.

Uther, seemed to feel his way without trouble and soon the sounds of laughter and conversation guided them to The Pub before they glimpsed the windows lit by candles which served to bring them in to safe harbour at the bar where they were received with gentle insults and rough, friendly slaps on the back.

Everybody feigned ignorance of the fact that Dylan was carrying a musical instrument, but somebody left the bar immediately he arrived and shortly thereafter a steady stream of irregulars made pilgrimage to The Pub in case some entertainment should be forthcoming.

Ignorant of the customs, Dylan laughed and drank with

the growing number of villagers that thronged about him, supposing this to be a regular feature of a night at The Pub until the moment that somebody asked if he would play a tune and silence fell like the blade of a guillotine that severed the threads of conversation and decapitated the head of steam that had been building up pressure with the anticipatory thrill that the guitar case had produced.

Dylan looked about at the sea of wide eyed, eager faces all brim full of hunger and hope and realised that even if his skills were as modest as he assessed them to be, it would be cruel beyond belief to deny this incipient audience some attempt at a show. The oppressive silence was rent with a collective exhalation like a dozen kettles reaching boiling point in unison as he reached for the guitar case and snapped the first catch.

If Dylan had considered the darkness to be a snug fit, it was as nothing to the palpable squeeze that the silence around him exerted as he tuned his guitar and mentally searched his repertoire for a suitable number with which to regale and nourish the culturally voracious citizens of Clae, as their paucity of song gnawed at them like any other hunger. So many required some frame of reference unavailable to the people present that he discarded them as soon as they surfaced in his consciousness, but they floated like flotsam, as he struggled for something to play. Then he realised that his guilty pleasure, his love of folk music was, under the current circumstances, the perfect solution.

The strings now tuned, possibly three times, as a bid to gain some thinking time, he began with a rendition of *John Barleycorn*. He was delighted at the reaction of his audience, some of whom were clearly recognising the theme and parts of the lyric, if their version differed a little in content.

He noted one man in particular had to restrain himself from attempting to sing along, so as Dylan finished a verse, he nodded encouragement to the fellow, who recognised and accepted the honour with a flush of colour to his face and an ecstatic burst of song just a little ahead of Dylan's guitar.

The audience now freed from the restraint shown as deference to their entertainer, now sang along and cheered as they gradually made this event their own, which also relieved the weight of responsibility that had pressed down upon Dylan as he no longer carried the entire evening upon himself. The singers and the guitar music gradually met and synchronised and too soon the song was done.

Dylan paused to take a drink and to consider the next tune when a cry of "Again!" was heard, adopted as a mantra and repeated until the guitar once again began the song from its beginning; so the chant was dissipated by song as the whole room took up the singing and all Dylan need do was to play, giving him time to plan the next song, *The Irish Rover*.

So the evening passed and the people forgot for a short time that their world had changed and that the dry bed of the river threatened more than their way of life, but the fragile balance that had suspended Clae between the sixteenth and twenty first centuries for so long.

It was Athena Slough who eventually broke up the event, not by evicting the crowd or closing The Pub, but as she saw signs of fatigue in Dylan as his enjoyment was gradually displaced by a pressing need for some rest, she took Dylan firmly by the arm and removed him and his guitar from The Pub and out onto the warm damp night.

There was a grateful cheer for Dylan's contribution as he was steered through the door and the relative quiet he left behind was soon enlivened by the strains of that first singer, again bellowing out the local version of *John Barleycorn*.

His guitar safely stored in its case, Dylan and Athena sat and listened to the singing behind them in the pub where undaunted by the loss of musical accompaniment, the regular and the less regular visitors continued the evening of song.

Uther and Desdemona joined them along with a few other influential members of the community, making a show of it being a casual meeting, but Athena shuffled closer to Dylan as if protecting him, and he gradually felt uneasy as the group focussed their attention on him and one after another they cleared their throats and said nothing beyond "How do?" and "Lovely evening!" or to compliment him on his entertainment.

Eventually it was Desdemona who spoke with her usual and honest method of making a decisive cut to the chase.

"We need somebody who knows the world outside to go and see if the River Henry can be restored, and we think ye are the man for the job."

Dylan blinked rapidly as he considered the prospect of leaving so soon, but he looked at the faces a round him and realised how ill equipped they would be to manage what they would encounter outside of the cloistered environs of Clae.

"Are ye up to the task?" Desdemona persisted, understanding what it was she was asking and looking at Athena with a silent apology as she pressed the young man for a response.

Dylan bowed his head and spoke. "I'm the obvious choice for the job!" he said, "Yes, I'll do it"

The relieved group of elders all thanked him and quickly made excuses to retreat, leaving Dylan reeling and morose about the prospect.

Dylan looked about him into the restful dark and realised that the same feeling was upon him as earlier when he had met and exchanged silences with the reticent beekeeper; it was one of feeling that the world he knew before arriving here had somehow been the dream, and this was the reality, where life was lived as it was meant to be lived, slowly, thoughfully and with care. If it wasn't for the dry bed of the River he would not even consider trying to adjust to that world when he knew that such a place as Clae existed and welcomed him, if the rest of the world was a dream then he was happy to have awoken.

Something in the sky moved and as he focussed on it, he saw it was a winking light on an aircraft high above them making its way to another country, another centre of modern life, and he sighed with his resigning himself to having to leave this place.

Athena saw all of the emotions passing across his face by the light of the moon, but she could only guess at the meaning behind them, though she liked the fact that Dylan was poor at concealing the passage of his thoughts and would make a terrible liar, which was yet another point in his favour. Athena herself had developed the diplomat's poker face in response to the demands of her duties, but she reasoned that Dylan could come to know her well enough to see past the diplomat's mask and see the real emotion dancing behind it, if only circumstances permitted the chance for them to know one another.

"What are ye thinking about?" she asked him softly, putting her arm through his and leaning into him as if wanting to share his warmth.

"I was just sad at having to leave this place. The world I go back to is a different, less developed place."

"Less developed?" Athena questioned, "I thought there were many wonders to be seen; I was almost curious enough to come with ye."

The look of horror that passed unbidden across Dylan's face was more than enough to convince Athena of his sincerity, so she assured him that Clae was her home, until he relaxed the tension she had felt in his arm and shoulder.

As Dylan almost dozed in this idyllic scene he heard Athena whisper something that he could barely make out.

"Come back to me." She had said "Don't leave me here without ye."

The night blew a warm moist air over them for a few

minutes before Dylan replied...

"There is no me, without you." He whispered. Athena splashed a few salty drops onto his shoulder, thankful and regretful at once, as he was preparing to leave.

Chapter Thirteen

Dean Baxter had followed his benefactor through woodland until they had reached a small and very rude hut set into a hillside and covered in twigs and leaves to the point of virtual invisibility, so that unless you knew what you were looking for, there was nothing to see but a tangle of vegetation. Inside the hut was little in the way of comfort but there were some utensils and a few large plastic storage boxes. It all reminded Baxter of a time he had spent camping with his Uncle Norman who enjoyed a sort of paramilitary camping experience, trapping wildlife for meals, and building rough shelters. Baxter viewed the shelter with approval and perhaps a little excitement.

His host gestured for Baxter to sit down on a hay bale set against the wall for that purpose, so Baxter sat and watched the deliberate movements of the other man as he shuffled about the place gathering items together to prepare a light meal.

He opened a hessian sack and peered inside, grunting with irritation at what he found. He turned a baleful eye on Baxter and said, "Wait here" before taking himself and the sack out of the hut and away.

Baxter looked about with a burning curiosity but more

than just a little fear of the tenant of this hovel kept him seated for a good ten minutes after the departure of the older man. There was plenty about his surroundings to occupy his attention. The hazel poles that formed the frame of the dwelling were bent to a central point where they were tied together. A tarpaulin sheet was the inner layer of the building, not the light artificial weave that is often used, but a heavy closely woven fabric of the old school. The outer shell was a collage of living ivy and willow with moss and leaves used to camouflage the whole building, considering the ample size of the room it was very well done.

    A few pots and pans, a jerry can and some tools were stacked just inside the doorway. A strange metal stove arrangement was built into a large clay mound at the back of the room against the hillside, the like of which Baxter had never seen. He wondered at the smoke from such a stove and wondered why somebody would take such trouble to hide themselves and then betray their location with a fire.

    The plastic storage boxes were translucent, and as such offered tantalising glimpses of the contents, but Baxter did not dare to open them and look. The Small cable drum that served as a table had a few items on it and one of these was a library book. The other articles on the table were a disposable pen and writing pad a pack of cards in a cardboard sleeve, a pair of thick glasses, and a large hunting knife.

    The knife, in a leather sheath, drew Baxter's eye time and again, until his curiosity got the best of him; with one eye on the entrance he reached out a trembling hand and slowly drew the knife from its home, he looked at the blade and saw that it was well used but kept clean and sharp. He felt it in his hand, the weight, the balance, turned the blade to reflect some light, and carefully put it back where he had found it.

    There it would have remained but at that moment he heard a squeal close by, making him start from his seat and without even a second thought he had the knife in his hand and was making for the doorway, such as it was.

    Once outside squinting in the sunlight, he tried to locate the source of the sound. It took him very little time to identify a rabbit caught in a snare not far from the shelter. Baxter licked his lips, nervously looking about, undecided on his course of action, but here he was with a rabbit in a snare, a hunting knife in his hand and the snare had obviously been set for a purpose, perhaps it was time to practice those skills that Uncle Norman had tried to teach him on their odd holidays.

    He butchered the rabbit and skinned it; he even found the frame to stretch out the skin for drying amongst the items beside the cooking pans.

Happy at his work and concentrating on the task, he was so absorbed that he failed to note the return of the man with the sack until his bulk was inserted between the sun and Baxter's work. Dean looked up frightened and was about to do what he usually did; to babble excuses, when the man dropped the now full sack beside him and bent over to peer at what Baxter was doing.

The merest ghost of a smile flashed across his dour features as he laid a rough dirt ingrained hand on Baxter's head.

"Good lad" he said before collecting the sack and taking into the shelter, leaving Baxter puzzled but more pleased than he would have expected at such scant approval. He correctly assumed that this was someone who did not waste words or deal out complimentary platitudes for the sake of massaging another's ego, but only on the rare occasions that somebody had managed to actually impress or please him.

The day passed amicably with small chores gradually weaving together to make a useful sort of a day of it, and by the time the evening came, the stove had made a miraculous and smokeless job of cooking the rabbit that Baxter had prepared and the new potatoes that were occupying the sack that had been empty that morning but on his return had been full of muddy, freshly dug, spuds.

The sun went down before they sat and ate in the warm damp air, when Baxter enquired why there was no smoke from the fire and the other explained the principle of the stove and how it utilised a system that captured the heat and the smoke output was minimal. The clay built up around the stove stored the heat and the stove pipe run through it before being allowed to escape outside almost at ground level.

One more surprise awaited Dean before this day was done; as darkness fell and he was jostled back into the shelter, he discovered there was another room, a bedroom which was dug into the hillside and panelled in wood. It was not a large room but afforded space enough for Baxter and his avuncular keeper to sleep without being too cosy.

It was a peaceful sleep that gradually fluffed up his thoughts and led them along increasingly unlikely paths until he was adrift in unconsciousness with a slight smile, as guileless as he had once been before acne and bitterness had transformed him.

During the early morning, before the sun had really put any effort into usurping the darkness and remained a glow of potential on the horizon, an armada of cloud came in from the sea and deposited its impressive payload across the downs, across the plains and the hills surrounding Clae on its way to assail the sleeping village with a downpour.

The rhythmic drumming of fat raindrops on the canvas roof of the bender tent couldn't breach the roof, but the sound they made managed to permeate the membrane of Baxter's unconsciousness and insinuate themselves chaotically upon his previous happy dreamscape as a threatening sound, like that of running feet, gunfire or war drums. The message that dragged him from the comfortable reverie was one of urgency and danger, but as his eyes flicked open and his unfamiliar surroundings and the absence of light exacerbated his fear, Baxter sat upright and gasped in the space between awaking and recollection of his circumstances.

The void was soon filled with an inrush of pieces of memory that within seconds were a coherent pattern; his next thought was for his guide, but a tentative arm extended beside him revealed that he was alone and that the cool spot nearby had been unoccupied for time enough for the body heat to have dispelled.

Beginning to panic, Baxter got to his knees and pulled back the canvas divide, to see if it revealed the man behind the curtain, but the main room, although it contained better lighting through its open vents, there was nobody there either.

A lightning flash cast strange jagged shadows that flickered and moved rapidly like images in a Zoetrope, before the thunder clapped in a darkness more profound after the whitewash of electrical flash.

Abject fear gripped the heart of Dean Baxter, and he tensed, rigid and immobile in the darkness and in anticipation or dread of another thunderclap, as the rain hissed and drummed on the roof and walls of the shelter.

Another flash and there in the doorway was a huge figure of a man holding a heavy staff silhouetted against the flashing sky, and almost simultaneously a clap of thunder sounded so loud that it was felt through the ground and made Baxter moan aloud with terror.

The figure entered the shelter and Baxter too afraid to move, just watched as the shape moved by feel about the room and lit a match with his back to Baxter and then turned holding a small oil lamp.

By the light of the lamp, Dean Baxter could see it was his host, soaked and grinning with a perverse amusement at the young man's terror. The weapon he held in his hand was a shovel, and as Dean's eyes fell to this object, the other man noticed his interest and spoke,

"When ye have to go, ye have to go; whatever the

weather". It was at this point that Dean realised that he did indeed, have to go, and it was perhaps only his catatonic fear that had saved him from an involuntary, inconvenient and wholly inappropriate action when the storm had begun.

With some urgency and without proper clothing he grabbed the shovel and headed off into the rain, but not too far that he would lose sight of his shelter from the storm. Even over the deafening splatter of rain against the woodland and the cracks of thunder he could hear the laughter that rang from the shelter, and despite his initial ire, it was not long before a smile broke his irritation and a small chuckle heralded the approach of a little perspective.

By the time he returned to the hut, the other man had prepared a small fire in his odd clay and metal stove, the room was already warming up and a blanket was provided with which to dry himself, while the smells of a breakfast soon made the earthy shelter feel comfortable and secure.

Chapter Fourteen

Hiawatha wasn't running away from Clae, he wasn't even running as he made his way carefully along the old route of the footpath, through well established nettles, bramble and briar, nutty hazel thickets and rocky uneven ground heading sharply upward to the serrated lip of the hilltop where the Clae sun first peeked over each morning to cast a benevolent glow across this favoured spot. The worst weather often made no effort to cross the hills the way the faithful sun would, each morning, clamber over Clae on its way towards Wales, Ireland and eventually to the Americas, long after it had dipped below the western hills casting its sanguine glow across the eastern hillside as it went.

No, Hiawatha wasn't running away from Clae, he was running towards an adventure as he crossed the hilltops and made his way down the other side, where the hunched trees and nettles seemed to grow thicker than ever. At last he came to an abandoned van off the road and made his way with tremulous wondering to the wreck. He ran his hand over the faded legend 'Lucky Sid's Chip's and Kebab's', pausing to ponder the identity of Lucky Sid and wonder what it was that had earned the wonder fuelled sobriquet. He would have been aghast at the truth; that it was a nickname, an ironic moniker for a character who was blessed with lots of luck and all of it bad, but cursed with a sense of fun so broad that these life experiences made him all the more cheerful as he chalked each disaster up on his mental scoreboard and considered every one of these adventures the inevitable knocks that he had to encounter in a life so full as his. Another business scheme which failed only in longevity, though it had passed all of his expectations as an escapade, so the venture lived on in legend, as well as in Sid's glorious memories and the faded lettering on the side of the van he had sold to Dylan when he saw the young man was on his own adventure and needed the van to get there.

    Hiawatha was almost defeated by the door latch but he found the mechanism eventually, though as he opened the passenger door he recoiled at the old cooking smells that lingered still, in the shell of a vehicle battered inside long before the bodywork was dented for the first time.

    It was clear that anything worth reclaiming had been taken by a person or persons who had noticed the van since it came to its final resting place. Still Hiawatha gazed at it, as he had grown up accustomed to metal being a precious resource and road vehicles being exclusively the occupants of books; as ethereal as the Minotaur and as difficult to understand when faced with one of the beasts who had previously only enjoyed the occasional, blurred existence of a child's imagination.

So much metal also lent a legendary quality to the device; an equivalent experience would be if you or I had stumbled on a fairy carriage made entirely of gold, with winged horses to draw it.

Such a signpost served to push him onward for greater rewards and the wonders awaiting his adventure; he coveted those experiences yet to come with an exquisite tortured anticipation, as detached and calm as a child on the eve of a birthday celebration. Even so, the fading light encouraged him to take shelter in the van's cavernous interior and continue at first light.

He considered his letter to Collitt and hoped it could convey his affection and his need to adventure, but he was still frightened at what the future may hold and concerned that he had left so much behind him.

He struggled to settle in the damp condensation laden atmosphere of the van with its alien smells and echoes of his every movement. Eventually he slept fitfully until the ringing of the first rainfall woke him in the early dawn, encouraging him to begin his journey to the new world and adventure. By the time he had gathered himself for the journey, the storm was upon him, the thunder claps were making the ground shake as he shook with tremulous thrills of excited imaginings of a world of possibilities that awaited him. It was not yet light enough to see his way but the heavens lit up with lightning and he was offered light for a second or two to show him the route he must take to get onto the highway that would take him to his destiny.

Amid this grand orchestration of impressive weather he strode purposefully and smiling into a brand new chapter of his life; the rain lashing his face reminding him that THIS was life, and he was living it.

The rain was still falling relentlessly and the respite it offered had be seized by an enthusiastic crowd of villagers who had put out anything which could contain water to fill with the sweet rain. Shylock Giza was keeping the sluices closed and watching the millpond replenish with the look of somebody whose faith in the providence of life was being vindicated with every life giving drop that fell into his pool.

It was a sombre group that gradually assembled in the Manor House that morning, after the music and song of the previous night. This group had come to see Dylan off on his mission to rescue the river and as they assembled there was a tangible gravity exerting a downward force on the mood. The storm that had awoken the village was all but passed, leaving just the rainfall in its wake.

Dylan looked about him hoping that one face in particular would be there and sure enough Desdemona Pippin did arrive with her sidekick, Athena, in close orbit, still concerned for her wellbeing. Desdemona, who had grown accustomed to being the one doing the looking after and made a terrible patient, kept waving her arm in Athena's general direction as if swatting at a fly.

Dylan smiled at Athena and picked up his guitar case. He held it out to her, but she looked confused, looking at the others for a clue about what this gesture could mean.

"Please look after this for me until I get back" said Dylan with raised eyebrows and a questioning expression that leant significance to his request.

Athena blushed and stepped forward to take the case with both arms and to cradle it as if it were the most precious of objects.

"I will be here..." she began and quickly corrected to "It will be here when ye get back" which satisfied Dylan as he planned to travel very light, so his pack had been left with Uther but his guitar was now safe in Athena's care.

At this point Collitt Semper came bursting through the doors clutching a damp note. With wordless anguish he extended the note for others to read what he was unable to articulate.

Uther gently took the note from the proffered hand and examined it carefully but the rain had taken its toll on the handmade paper and the sooty ink, to the point that nothing could be read of the streaks that once were words. The tear streaked face of Collitt was as crumpled as the sheet but he was gradually regaining his breath and the words came between sobs.

"Hia – watha… gone… left… the.. village!".

Hiawatha's parents, Daisy and Nebuchadnezzar, simultaneously gasped in shock, moving to stand one either side of Collitt to support him and to commiserate.

Desdemona turned to Dylan and he took a step backwards in fear that he would be blamed for bringing stories of the outside world to disturb the status quo, but it was with concern and a solitary question that she addressed him.

"What will happen to him?" she asked simply. Dylan shook his head slowly and stated truthfully that he could not guess what may happen to him, while considering with an inward flinch the probable fate of a naive young man in the cruel world he had left.

His inability to keep his emotions from his face meant

that Athena was on him in an instant.

"Ye think he is in danger don't ye?" she demanded with a mild accusatory tone. Again Dylan flinched but nodded sadly.

Dylan found himself considering human nature and although he considered himself to be an optimist, his outlook was far bleaker than the views held by the people of Clae who felt that everyone was essentially wonderful and behaviour like that exhibited by Baxter was seriously aberrant and unusual. In arguing that all people can behave in an equally appalling fashion, had he become the serpent in Eden?

With a shock he realised that he was probably a poison in the life of the village, a toxin to corrupt the fresh atmosphere of the village not just with awakening the curiosity of the young and adventurous, but by bringing his scepticism into an environment where such opinions are not reflected in the behaviour of the indigenous folk.

Desdemona was considering the situation and when she spoke it was with nods of approval from all of the elders.

"Please find him and make sure he is safe" she pleaded. Dylan still preoccupied with his dark assessment of his influence was slow to grasp the change of priorities.

"The river…" he began

"…Can wait" interrupted Uther. Desdemona agreed,

"Look after Hiawatha first" she told him.

Without preamble or hesitation, Dylan picked up the small bag he planned to take and with a last look at Athena, he turned on his heel and headed back out of the village in the approximate direction he had entered it.

Athena watched him leave, haunted by the finality of his look. Guitar, or no guitar, she had a feeling that she had seen the last of him and something inside of her began to shrivel, something that had been growing almost unawares within her, and something like mourning washed over her to the point that she almost followed him, but for the hand of Desdemona on her arm.

Desdemona looked at her sternly.

"Will he come back to us?" asked Athena in a small voice.

"Hiawatha or Dylan?" asked Uther: at which Desdemona shot him a withering glance and silently mouthed a sympathetic "Oh!" in response. Desdemona returned her attention to Athena.

"I don't know" she answered truthfully, "but I think he is smart enough to find his way home."

Athena wanted desperately to be comforted by that but even as he disappeared from view, Dylan did not so much as cast a backwards glance at the place he was leaving with the intention of never setting foot in the village again. Much as he detested the modern world, there was nothing that could tempt him to pollute the idyll he had discovered, even unintentionally. His very presence represented a risk he was unwilling to take.

    Hiawatha had travelled a few miles before Dylan had even set off, and as the sun rose he saw the lights of the distant town slowly fade. As he approached the town he saw the skyline through the trees and marvelled at such huge buildings, with so much glass.

    It was about this time that his hunger began to insist it was paid some attention, so he looked about him to see what may be available. A drystone wall ran alongside the road he was following so he peeped over the wall at the field which spread below the height of the road on the other side.

    A mildly surprised sheep looked back at him with huge unblinking eyes. In the field beyond he could see a track leading to a farmhouse, with a garden. He could see the unmistakable signs of a vegetable garden there and thought it would be a good place to find some refreshment. Hopping over the wall he made for the farmhouse across the field.

    The building was in good repair, the farmyard had lots of

metal equipment laying about, all of which fascinated and puzzled Hiawatha. The labour intensive methods employed in Clae included no tractors or balers and even the modern harrow was a curiosity to Hiawatha. He approached the farmhouse with some trepidation and knocked at the door. There was no answer and he discovered that the door would not open. It was in a state of good repair and unlikely to be stuck, so he assumed it must be stopped on the other side. Perhaps another door was the one in use. He circled the building and came to the vegetable garden at the rear of the property, his mouth watering at the sight of fresh lettuce in a neat row on a raised bed. He picked a few outer leaves from the first plant, folded them and took a bite with his eyes closed in appreciation of the juice and the flavour.

"You look like you're enjoying my lettuce" said a voice behind him.

Hiawatha jumped with surprise and turned to face the man who has caught him out, but he was busy chewing and unable to make any reply. To his surprise the face wasn't angry or threatening, in fact he seemed amused at Hiawatha's situation.

The relative age that it takes to chew and swallow when there is a need to speak, was extended by the awkwardness of the situation and it was only the patient manner in which the farmer awaited his response that allowed Hiawatha to swallow without choking.

"I am sorry" he managed eventually, "I was so hungry and I couldn't find somebody to ask"

"Not to worry" said the farmer, looking at the young man's rough clothing and assessing him to be a vagabond, "I've been famished myself once or twice. Now if you don't mind a little work, I can feed you before and after it"

Hiawatha nodded eagerly and was soon sitting at the kitchen table whilst the farmer cooked up some bacon and eggs with some bread that tasted different to any bread that he had ever tasted. He suspected that their miller was not the man that Shylock Giza was and that the flour was at fault, but he said noting and chewed on the tasteless stuff all the same. He declined the tea he was offered and sank a pint of water instead, it tasted odd as if it had been left in a bucket and taken the taint of metal, bet the farmer smiled as though he approved of this choice of refreshment.

The barn was his place of work and when the farmer saw him tackle the pile of dung with a fork and a barrow, he was confident enough to leave him to it while he got on with his morning's work.

At lunchtime the barn was cleaned with straw down on the floor. A friendly woman walked in and looked about with some surprise.

"Good work" she smiled, "Joe said you will be joining us for lunch, so clean up at the tap and come on in the house"

Hiawatha stepped out of the barn into the continuing rain, looked about for a place to wash, saw a water butt outside the house and washed himself there before he made his way to the door, pausing only to take off his boots in the porch before venturing inside.

Joe the farmer was in the kitchen with the woman who had called him, both of them moving about one another in a slow dance refined by years of practice, in which he would add a little salt to this pan while she chopped some herbs behind him, and then they would swap places effortlessly without collision but seemingly without looking to see where the other was at the time. By the time they paid any attention to Hiawatha, the meal was ready to be served, and dishes of vegetables were being put onto the table and he was bustled into chair and a pint pot of water placed in front of him. Joe sat opposite with a similar pint, and looked at his young employee across the dishes.

"What's your name lad?" he asked with a smile.

"Hiawatha, Sir. Hiawatha Longfellow"

Joe looked sharply at him to see if there was a hint of sarcasm or mischief in his demeanour, but he saw only the guileless candour of a naive young man, looking clear eyed back at him, so he laughed, and the woman laughed with him.

"Hello Hiawatha! I'm Sally" the woman told him, "and this is Joe"

Joe nodded his affirmation and started to ladle boiled potatoes onto his guest's plate. Hiawatha was impressed with the smooth china plates and the metal cutlery; he was also impressed with the quantity and tastes of the food before him.

There was so much to take in, from the cooker that seemed to make heat without a fire, to the little lights on almost every piece of equipment, and the cord that each item was secured with, perhaps as a means of preventing them being removed.

The textures of the tablecloth and the plate were smoother than he was accustomed to, but his attention kept coming back to the food. Beside him on the worktop was a bowl of fruit, apples and pears he recognised but the strange curved yellow objects and the green and orange coloured one with a spiky green tuft on top were alien to him. His eye was drawn back to the bowl time and again, so that his gaze was noticed and interpreted as covetous hunger, so that after the meal, Joe took two bananas and gave one to Hiawatha and began to peel the other himself.

Hiawatha copied the peeling process and soon was biting into the flesh of a banana for the first time in his life. It was strange to him to feel a texture that was first like a soft pear but consistent throughout, no core or change of texture as he bit through it. Then he had the soft sweet flavour of the banana assailing his senses with its almost dizzying aroma. He closed his eyes to savour the experience and Joe and Sally exchanged smiles as they assumed it had been a while since the young man had enjoyed a piece of fruit.

The friendly couple offered him more work, but the town and adventure beckoned him to move on. So armed with a bag of apples and another banana, he said a cheerful farewell to the farm and moved on down the road.

He had not gone far when the farmer's wife ran through the rain to catch him up and slipped a piece of smooth paper into his hand.

"This is the address of a friend of mine, if you need a place to stay" she said kindly, before turning back to the house with a cheerful wave. The piece of paper was pushed carefully to the bottom of his bag to keep it dry. He smiled at the warmth of the couple and set his eyes again in the direction of the town.

The rain was still falling hard as Hiawatha resumed his journey along the road at the same time as Dylan reached the wrecked van and saw that it had been stripped of its contents. He set out on the road to town afoot, unaware that Hiawatha was only about an hour ahead of him.

Chapter Fifteen

Burma Conduit and her friend Athena Slough usually met up in the shade of a willow tree on the crossroads after their day's work was done to share news and thoughts. On this occasion they met earlier than usual due to the unusual circumstances, though the steady rain discouraged lingering too long, even under the modest cover of the willow's branches.

Burma had taught Athena to read and write, but the student had soon overtaken the teacher and Burma had delighted in Athena's voracious reading and sharp intelligence, fuelling her passion for learning by putting more and more in her path. Athena could not underestimate the influence of Burma's enthusiastic participation in her learning, as she had soon attracted the attention of Ben Caliban and Desdemona, both of whom individually recognised her potential and both quietly sponsored her position as an apprentice to Uther and as the next matriarch.

Out of all of this developed a deep affection between the two women and a shared love of learning. Even the dry tomes in Ballentine's library would eventually be called upon to satisfy their continuing desire for new material, and the favourite volumes had been carefully read and re-read on numerous occasions.

Hopes, aspirations, and nightmares were shared between the two of them whenever they met, to the point that they held back little from each other while oft times, the telling the of the tale was a superfluity of communication, as the subtle signals had already been sent and received by the time they were close enough to be heard. The posture, the stride, expression, the blunt forthright content of the eyes, in the context of their daily exchange would tell the other all they needed to know before a single clumsy word, or gross sentence attempted to capture what had already been perceived.

Therefore as they met, it was a tearfully emotional Burma who held out her arms to an outwardly stoic Athena who walked stiffly but unresisting into the embrace.

Athena's long dark hair shrouded her face as she buried it in Burma's shoulder, she allowed herself a single sob, and prolonged the embrace until both women felt revitalised by it. Burma knew Athena well enough to be unimpressed by the dryness of her eyes and the set of her jaw as they stood apart, she saw the anguish beneath the marble, smooth, cold, hard, surface of her composure. Too much for her friend to bear she consoled herself by gathering Athena in her arms again and hugging her until her own feelings were almost under control.

Burma knew that something needed to be done to

distract Athena and she also knew that their shared love of puzzles may be the answer.

"What can we do about the River?" she asked.

Athena stepped back and regarded her friend quizzically, wondering from where the question had arisen, but quickly spotting the ploy decided to see if it was indeed the panacea that Burma hoped by immersing herself in it for a while, either way it would be enjoyable and perhaps helpful.

"The route under the hills would be dry now" Burma reasoned, "perhaps it would be possible to follow it back and see if it is stopped somewhere along."

Athena shook her head.

"Too dangerous." She said "Uther would never allow it"

"What if Uther didn't know" asked Burma, and for a second they made silent eye contact and then laughed at the absurdity of risking their lives without informing anyone of their plan, or indeed, of going against the wishes of the elders.

"The thing that puzzles me, is why the Henry should be dry and Pinnock's Paddock, flooded." muttered Athena, almost to herself.

"One of the puzzling things about Pinnock's Paddock, is why The Emperor would make such a point of declaring himself to be the protector of The West Paddock in the first place."

At fist Athena frowned at this apparent non sequitur, but then another idea struck her. Perhaps there was a relationship between these two aspects of the paddock, and an answer may be found. At the same moment she realised that Burma was correct about the puzzle; not only was it a welcome distraction, it was exciting.

"Perhaps there is something about the West Paddock that The Emperor kept a secret" she suggested.

Burma's eyes lit up with the possibilities that filled her head.

"Treasure?" she asked.

"I don't know" replied Athena, "but I want to find out."

"Then we should start at the library" said Burma already striding in the direction of the Manor house.

In one of the quiet corners of Clae, not that there is any other kind, is the home of Apollo Brokken, as yet only a child, but showing promise for the future. Not the promise of living up to his name, for that forlorn hope his diminutive parents are responsible, if responsible is a word that can aptly describe people inclined to bestow an appellation like "Apollo" on a beloved child.

Despite a name he was genetically unequipped to live

up to, he was a bright child, and flattered Burma Conduit's teaching skill with his interest in most subjects, and in particular his fascination with history.

The historical Brokken, was perceived by young Apollo, not so much as the distant Saxon forbear who once held the tract of land where Clae now stands, but as one might perceive an uncle that has been often discussed around the meal table but never greeted in person.

In the days of the historical Brokken, Clae was a gift from the Gods, naturally fortified by the sharp rocky outcroppings that castellated the surrounding hills. The hills themselves had attracted the kind of plant life that tore scratched and stung anyone foolish enough to attempt passage. The natural security offered by the region was not wasted on that Chieftain of old. He set up his little community and it settled down to endure, and endure it does.

Apollo knew all of this, and he had seen Brokken's sword where it hung above the mantle in the library. He had even managed to get Ballantine Trimble to whisper what he knew about the heroic figure.

For Apollo, the fact that he had been given Brokken's name made him feel closer in time and kinship to his ancient forefather. He had a tenuous grasp of the distance between them, measured in a surprisingly small number of generations. There was a book in the library, which held all of the begats from Clae's first day that gave him his understanding. Though many assumed the list to be partly historical and fading into the apocryphal, there was a good feeling of solid continuity that anchored the locals to this micro republic, and gave them a sense of belonging that was perhaps only really understood by other tribal folk, which gave the denizens of Clae a closer kinship with the Maasai of Amboseli or the Australian aborigine than the English people who lived close by but relatively rootless.

Apollo expanded his own knowledge with detailed study of the documents and records he could find in the library of the Manor House where Ballentine Trimble had grown accustomed to his regular presence, but did not object because he was essentially an agreeable chap. He also found Apollo to be a quiet study and recognised the reverence that Apollo held for the library; of that too he approved.

So it was that when Burma and Athena burst in on the library, it was Apollo that they disturbed, while Ballentine was elsewhere making tea for Mavis and whispering his growing affection.

Apollo had no desire to be in the way, so he quickly

excused himself and prepared to leave, while the two women began to search for the information that could lead them to the answer they sought. Burma was always sensitive to the people she taught, so she assured Apollo that he was not in the way. He moved to a quiet corner and reluctantly remained until he was again lost in his research.

The women had knowledge of the library content that was extensive but not exhaustive as was Ballentine's, so they were soon faced with an impasse where the information they hoped to find was apparently not on open display and must, if it is there to be found, reside in the cubby holes, drawers or cabinets that filled every inch of wall space that wasn't shelved and resplendent with the gilt lettering of several generations of books gathered by collectors who must have had these volumes ferried in along the footpath in the days when it was regularly travelled. Nothing new had graced these shelves since an influx of the mass-market paperback volumes had followed *Lost Horizons* into one corner of the library, these relatively delicate, slender books, sit apart from their grander counterparts, the poor relations of the printed world, the literary proletariat, not just James Hilton, but P.G. Wodehouse, Agatha Christie, Zane Grey and others cluster together trying to keep their spines straight to stand up to the bigger books, but so few in number and being more roughly treated by the passage of years than the robust leather covers of the solid tomes about them, they looked their age, with the youngest of them having arrived in the mid 1930s.

However it was the forgotten older contents of the library that were of interest at this point, those vellum sheets, more ancient and fragile than the appearance of the pariah paperbacks. Those scrolls and manuscripts that they felt must be hidden in some unexplored case, and hold the answer to the riddle of The West Paddock.

"Have ye found anything at all?" asked Burma as she ran a finger along the spines of books in a dark corner that she had seldom visited, trying hard to make sure she took in and weighed every title for its usefulness to the quest.

"Hmmm!" replied Athena, beginning to become absorbed in what was in front of her on a desk.

"What have ye found?" Burma moved to stand beside her friend and peer over her shoulder at the hand written volume at which she gazed.

Unable to get close enough to properly read the scrolled handwriting, she was growing impatient to know what was on the page, but Athena was still reading and not yet willing to speak of her discovery, until she abruptly moved to one side and offered Burma the chance to get closer.

Burma looked at the open page and scanned rapidly down the verso, then with growing disappointment down the recto.

"This is all about Brokken!" she said with an edge of irritation in her voice, at which point Apollo's head snapped up from his transcribing of a passage of interest, and began to take an interest in the activities of the two women.

Athena summarised what she had read.

"That is a diary of his studies kept by Fulmin Pinnock. It seems he thought there was a treasure here somewhere, the secret of Brokken's power."

Apollo spoke up at this point unable to restrain himself from sharing his enthusiasm for the almost mythic forbear whose name he proudly bore.

"He was a powerful warrior, and kept Clae safe for his whole life."

Burma knew of Apollo's interest and could not dismiss his comment, as she followed up on his remark more from habit than fascination.

"How did he manage to protect the village?" she asked.

"It is written…" said Apollo looking wide eyed about him to indicate in a general sense where it was written "It is written that he had a treasure that would protect the village in its time of greatest need, and that no army had managed to take the lands of Clae since Clae himself had taken them and called them after himself."

Athena was now interested, so she followed up with a question of her own.

"Who was Clae?" she asked moving closer to Apollo lest the disrespectfully raised voices should attract the attention of Bally Trimble, eager to keep the sanctity of the library from being desecrated by noise.

Apollo fairly glowed to be quizzed on his favourite topic and was happy to relate what he knew of the legendary Norse giant who had stamped down the land and threaded needles into the trees and plants in order to create a peaceful valley in which he may rest. The local demons feared him so greatly that they too agreed to patrol the woodland around the area but never to cross the hills and disturb the giant as he rested from his labours. When Clae decided that his time was done, he sadly left the secret sanctuary he had made and passed on to the feasting hall of his fellow immortals, passing on the district to the mightiest and wisest of the warriors of the old land to keep while the men of Rome, the men from the north, the Saxons, Normans, and the others tried and failed to take away this most precious tract of sacred earth.

Burma was impressed with his research but Athena was considering and filtering the content of the legend that could be allegory which may contain some kernel of historic detail that could aid their quest.

It was the serious thought that Athena was applying that alerted Burma to the fact that a clue may be found.

"I don't understand" she admitted, "Why was The Emperor so interested in Brokken?"

"Why indeed?" Athena agreed "Unless...."

"Unless he had discovered the secret of Brokken's power, the power of the Giant Clae"

Apollo nearly fell off his chair at the revelation.

"Ye mean there really is a secret, a treasure? There may be something that Brokken left, and it is here to be found?"

"It may be" allowed Burma "and ye may be the very man to help us with the search"

Brokken puffed out his chest and slapped it with an open hand. "Madam! I am your knight, your chevalier, your servant" and with that he swept a theatrical bow.

Athena laughed kindly and turning to her friend she asked,

"What have ye been reading to them?"

Burma blushed a little but said nothing. Apollo smiled and kept her secret.

The trio settled down to find out what they could about Brokken, on the assumption that whatever Fulmin Pinnock XII, Emporer of Clae and protector of the West Paddock had discovered, he probably discovered it here in the library first and the information was there for others to find. It was possible that The Emperor had recorded his findings somewhere in his own writings so the search was now to find anything they could about the Mythical Clae, the legendary Brokken and the almost legendary Fulmin Pinnock XII.

Chapter Sixteen

Hiawatha made his way along the road at the steady pace of one who is used to this mode of transportation and is comfortable with his own ability, in that he is able to accurately assess the pace he needs to set in order that he may keep it up all day.

The sun arced across the sky and was dipping towards the buildings of the town as he passed the outlying houses and started to wrinkle his nose at the smells about him. The fumes of the vehicles he had accepted as they passed him along the road wafting the acrid smell of burned fuel in their wake. He had breathed so much of that it no longer made such an unpleasant impression upon him as the vehicles became more frequent and the air contained the omnipresent taint of their fetid breath.

It was other smells that he found hard to deal with. A sewerage treatment plant with the wind behind it blew the stench of human excrement across his path, which stopped him in his tracks and caused him to wonder what manner of animal was nearby and question its health.

As he passed the verges frequented by dog walkers their leavings also reached his sensitive nostrils, and he was amazed to see the pretty colours of items in the hedgerows and on verges but soon realised that these were manmade objects in disrepair. Some of them were made of stiff heavy paper and brightly coloured, which caused him to wonder who Macdonald might be and why he should claim ownership of these damaged containers. Other names and other colours decorated these items that in other settings and other circumstances he may have found beautifully decorated in such vivid colours, and emblazoned with strange designs and different lettering styles, some stylised to the point of being arcane.

So absorbed was he by the fascinating detritus of this culture that he failed to note that it had stopped raining at last, and the light was fading. He carried along the roadside with his steady stride, still looking this way and that, at the many commonplace items that were things of wonder to this stranger from paradise unable to differentiate the sacred from the profane, and seeing splendour in detritus and unable to see the fast moving, foul smelling vehicles as revered symbols of status, personality and freedom that lifted their status to the sacred in this society.

As the sun finally sank below the false horizon of the skyline, he was amazed at the light that sprang into being about him. By now he had followed the main road into the town centre and the lights coming on in shop windows lit up these boxes of delights that displayed such items whose purpose he could only guess at. He spent a long time trying to guess what some of these things were for and then he happened to pass an electrical goods store which had an array of TV sets in the window, all displaying a broadcast channel or an advertising loop. He stared open mouthed at first, finding the array of images all too much to absorb. After a while he found that each screen showed a different themed set of images, so by concentrating on one screen at a time, he was able to imagine a story unfolding: on one screen was a woman in splendidly ornate but old fashioned clothes, who seemed to spend a lot of time walking through fields lined with hedgerows. It was apparent that she was interested in the activities of a man who rode a horse and wore similarly ornate old fashioned clothing and lived in a house like the Manor House of Clae; a thought that gave him a pang of regret at leaving.

 Another screen showed a series of apparently unconnected images, first a scene of people wearing robes and carrying large black metal objects close to their chests. There were pictures of families looking frightened and dust or smoke drifted through the scenery. Hiawatha knew enough about the weapons to appreciate that that is what the people were cradling in their arms, so he considered that the war hadn't ended, but moved to another land to assail another people, and bring fear and misery to another corner of the world that longed for peace the way the people of Clae had longed for it when the explosions shook the ground at night and sometimes during the day. He shuddered visibly and turned his attention to another screen on which a woman wearing a red clinging dress was pointing at a map which moved and changed as she pointed at it, so that as she indicated the north of the British Isles, so the image grew larger to emphasise the region, she passed her hand over it and arrows indicated the direction of her gesture, then small raindrops fell across the map like a drawing of rainfall.

 Hiawatha drew his coat about him and looked up at the sky and could see the stars above him, somehow faded and weaker than usual, the sky not as dark, and it frightened him a little to see the peaceful darkness compromised like this. He realised that the rain had passed and decided to move along and find a place to rest for the night and somewhere to sit and eat the apples he had carried since the farm. Besides which he found that his concentration or the flickering of the images was beginning to make his head ache and he desired some respite.

 With no clear idea of how long he had watched the screens, he was starting to wonder where he might spend the night so he continued along the road in the same direction he had travelled most of the day.

He came to a junction at which there was a shop that was alive with activity, there was a warm food smell wafting on the night air and a crowd of teenagers standing outside, laughing, talking and eating.

Hiawatha was tempted to greet them as he would at home, but as he didn't know them or their customs he decided to walk past slowly to give them the opportunity to take a lead that he could follow.

A few of them nudged one another at his approach, nodding in his direction and pointing with a handful of food wrapping. As he came alongside the group, one of them stepped in his path.

"Here mate! You want some chips? I'm full and I'll only have to chuck 'em in the bin"

Hiawatha met the gaze of the young man who was holding out a wrapper to him opened like the petals of flower to reveal at the heart a golden array of hot greasy, delicious looking chips.

"Thank ye!" said Hiawatha reaching out to receive the chips. The other lad handed the packet over. Hiawatha tentatively took a chip and bit into it, only to find that it was tasty and hot, with a crispy skin that tasted a little like dripping.

The generous lad spoke first.

"I'm Graham, this is Clipper, over there is George, and this is Jenny, and there is Laura."

"I'm Hiawatha" he replied "It's good to meet ye all"

The conversation was centred around the evening's activities and Graham stood next to Hiawatha occasionally taking a chip from the wrapper making him realise that it was kindness that had prompted his open handed gesture, so Hiawatha made sure he took only a share of the chips and allowed his host to take a fair portion too. Graham also noticed the decency of this arrangement and found himself warming to the stranger.

"We're going to the youth club if you want to come along" offered Jenny putting her arm through Graham's affectionately. "It only costs fifty P"

"I don't have any peas" Hiawatha admitted, "but I have some apples" and to prove the point he opened the bag and offered them around. Everyone took one and thanked him, then Clipper spoke up with a mouthful of apple.

"We can get Hiawatha into the club can't we?"

Everyone signalled agreement, and Jenny linked her other arm through Hiawatha's and tugged at him gently to become part of the group.

They arrived at an old building with peeling paint on the door and window frames, It stood in contrast to its more modern neighbours, a sad relic awaiting demolition, given a stay of execution as a meeting place for new mothers during the morning, exercising pensioners in the afternoon and young people in the evening.

At the door a man wearing a white band around his neck and a long black gown performed a ritual with a few of the members of the group who each handed him some coins and in return he tore a small rectangle of paper from a book and handed these rectangles in exchange. As Clipper performed the ritual in front of him, Hiawatha was mildly excited to be handed one of these rectangles and slightly mystified to discover it had "G970" printed upon it. He followed Clipper through the door smiling at the man with the neck band as he passed.

The group had reassembled in a corner and as he approached them he heard Laura speaking.

"...and I bet he doesn't have anywhere to stay, poor sod!" as she said this she turned slightly and saw Hiawatha and Clipper approaching and flushed red as she became apparently transfixed by her shoes.

"Hey Hiawatha" called George "Do you have anywhere to

sleep tonight?"

Laura slapped him lightly and spoke his name in the manner of a rebuke.

"George!"

"It's a fair question" said George in his own defence.

"No I don't" said Hiawatha sheepishly but with a smile that suggested it was not a problem but conveyed to the others that it was probably not unusual.

"You can kip in my Dad's shed if you like" said George "He won't mind if he never finds out" and the others all laughed.

Music began to play from a music system somewhere near the trestle table set up as a drinks and snacks outlet and Hiawatha visibly jumped causing even more laughter from the others. After a few moments Hiawatha had decided that he preferred Dylan's guitar to the load rhythmic chanting and the incomprehensible lyrics of the music that was pumping out of the player.

Laura took his hands in hers and pulled him gently towards the open space in the middle of the room where nobody was standing or dancing.

"Let's dance" she shouted over the music.

Hiawatha was too polite to decline so he followed her

lead to the accompanying whooping of the others and assorted onlookers he copied her joyous movements about the dance floor, until his exuberance showed that he was having a lot of fun out there and the music began to make sense, as it had previously had no context. This was what it was for, not for tapping the feet or for singing along with, but to simply feel the rhythm and move with the sound.

 Irresistibly drawn to the fun he was obviously having, the other people gradually started to get onto the dance floor until the whole room was a mass of gyrating laughing teenagers leaping and calling out to friends to join in. The drinks stand did a great trade and Hiawatha danced until he could dance no more and collapsed laughing into a chair against the wall where Graham placed a cold drink in his hand and shouted to him that it was the best night they had ever spent at the youth club. When the music stopped, everyone was slapping Hiawatha on the back and women he had never met gave him a hug. It appeared he was destined to become something of a legend in this part of town, and the friends he had acquired were determined to make the most of it. The small band left together singing and jostling one another down the road until one by one they hugged each other or kissed each other on the cheek and filtered off to their respective homes until there was just George and Hiawatha, walking just behind a young woman that the latter notes is painfully thin.

George observing what his companion has seen said "Ugh! She has anorexia. I can't bear to look at her"

Hiawatha had never heard of anorexia but he was at a loss to feel anything but sad at George's comment as it was not her fault that she had the illness and George's unwillingness to interact with her seemed cruel to him as it suggested that George would only speak with people who were well. It took a few moments of contemplation, to imagine a world where people would be ostracised for their poor health but it defeated his efforts, as he could not imagine a community holding together with such harsh judgements being so casually applied. The curious soul who had wanted to explore this brave new world shrank away a little, retreated towards Clae, beginning to feel the ghost of the horror that had been unwittingly stamped on Dylan's countenance when he had first proposed this adventure.

    Down a side road, they went away from the last of the stragglers towards an unremarkable semi-detached brick house with a cosy garden shed where Hiawatha could sleep in safe exhaustion after the exertions of the day and a good portion of the night.

Clae

He lay with a blanket beside a lawnmower and some garden tools, listening to the distant sounds of occasional cars, TV sets, cats nocturnal activities and the light that remained even at this late hour and in a shed where the thick dust on the window failed to keep out a high level of residual light.

It was the lack of darkness more than anything else that disturbed Hiawatha, unsettled him and made him think fondly of home. He reasoned that perhaps he was just frightened and looking for excuses that justified his fears, but it was to the window that his eyes kept returning as if he could will that sickly orange light to go out and give the night over to its proper level of restful, darkness. The light seemed to permeate the world, to come from everywhere at once, it made the sky lighter and leaked in everywhere. He wondered for a moment if Clae was also bathed in this terrible luminance but assured himself that Clae was still Clae and it was night time there as it had always been. But many more minutes were passed looking wide eyed at the web skinned window before he was finally claimed by sheer exhaustion and slept the sleep of the over exuberant.

Chapter Seventeen

Dylan in his concerned haste, had not fared as well as Hiawatha in his passage through the teeth of Clae's protective band, he had emerged already worn down by his exploits and began his walk to town at a speed too great to maintain for long.

The first hour or so he was fixed on the horizon, his eyes scanning the road ahead and his thoughts all focussed on Hiawatha, but as he grew tired attempting to persist at a punishing pace, he was forced to slow down and catch his breath. As he slowed his thoughts wandered to other concerns: first he wondered how far he could get with the cash he had, which was a modest sum accumulated form a few months work prior to leaving town for adventure, though the adventure he had so far experienced was not on his plans at all. He thought of where he could sleep that night as he considered the cost of a hostel bed or a night on a park bench. He then wondered how he was supposed to track down an individual in a town this size, unless he was hospitalised or arrested, the thought of which spurred him to another concentrated burst of speed until he again succumbed to fatigue and had to reduce the pace.

"If only..." he chided himself "If only I had taken a little of the money from that sack. It was only then that it struck him that the sack, and the gun had not been seen or mentioned since the incident. He distinctly remembered that both had remained behind when they had left the scene of the drama, more concerned with Desdemona's health than trifling matters such as THOUSANDS OF POUNDS IN CASH and a LOADED PISTOL!

It was amazing how just being in Clae could twist his priorities into a sequence that pleased him more. Those virtues of honesty and cooperation that are expressed as the values of our society are easily overshadowed by the real motivators of action for the people who are held up by the media as inspirational figures on whom we should model our own aspirations. They exemplify the antithesis of the virtues we are supposed to admire when they succeed by virtue of aggression, competition, and acquisitiveness.

In Clae it was possible to rise to earn the esteem and admiration of the villagers by virtue of generosity of spirit, kindness, cooperation, honesty and kindness again, yes, above all else it was kindness, and kindness was the creed that replaced the New Testament of The Bible, by distilling all of the wisdom of the Sermon on the Mount. And ignoring allegory and allusion, taking the very heart out of the teachings and ignoring the superstition that clouds the issue in every major religion of the world, it came down to that one simple truth, kindness is the way to heaven, and you don't have to wait until you die to get there.

But what had become of the money and the gun? Who in Clae would have wanted them? Where had Baxter gone to after he fled the scene? It troubled Dylan to think that Baxter could have made his way back to the world outside and revealed something of the secret valley. Dylan felt like weeping when he pictured helicopters flying in news film crews and the bewildered residents being subjected to the stresses of the world, so that they needed to worry about taxes and work, utility bills and education, when none of things currently had the power to make even an indentation on the surface of the village. Work was how they survived, and they did it gladly for the communal good. Utilities were provided by the land or by that same hard work, and education was something which inevitably happens to a person as they travel through this life with a little curiosity and some free time to indulge it.

Despite his worries, or because of his preoccupation with them, the miles passed by with relative speed until he found himself on the town fringes and located a bus stop on one of the side roads where the local shuttle busses wove through the suburbs and looped through the town centre. The busses were never far apart and within ten minutes he saw one over the parked cars as it hove into sight. Sadly it was number 147 which he recalled went a long way to the town centre, but it was better than waiting longer and better than walking so he hopped on board and bought a ticket. Sitting by the window he saw the familiar sights of the town go by with a bitter sort of amusement at the contrast between here and the two streets of Clae.

The Dyer Distillery was a majestic brick monument compared to the corrugated metal walls of the Picking's Packing Company depot, and the little council estates looked rather like endless chevrons of holiday camp chalets in comparison with the stone crofts of Clae. Even the girls in contemporary clothing looked uncomfortable and awkward victims of their style compared to the homespun functional clothes worn by Athena.

Eventually the bus found its way onto the High Street, and past the unfortunate Coltsfoot and Briar Building Society building, down past the best chip shop in town where a group of teenagers were hanging about. Dylan imagined they were on their way to the youth club where the vicar would allow them to play dance music and drink orange squash.

He had no idea where to begin his search, so he hopped off by the Youth Club and walked on through the darkening streets until he found the area of town where the stores were still open and there was activity enough to attract a stranger seeking food and company. This was the part of town where many Caribbean people had settled in the fifties, and their legacy was this part of town with Soul Food cafes, Reggae clubs, music and light, people walking and shopping from market barrows even now as it got late. Dylan loved this part of town for its life and its friendly atmosphere; a white person with respect had nothing to fear in this street.

He walked from one end of the district to the other, stopping only for some saltfish and dumplings with some ginger beer to fortify himself and carry on his quest. A few familiar faces greeted him and he asked if any had seen the rough shirt and curly mop of hair that made Hiawatha stand out from the crowd a little, but nobody recalled having seen him.

Dylan finally came to rest in a cafe with a cup of coffee, and stared out of the window until the people walking past blurred and faded as he was gradually pulled down into a disturbed sleep. He dreamt of Hiawatha lost on the shores of Lake Superior, and he was searching, calling, as he walked on and on, but every time he saw Hiawatha he changed into an animal or a bird and disappeared into the trees. Eventually he became distressed and ran to the lake, to refresh himself and there in the water he saw Athena, her reflection rippling with the catspaw that disturbed the water's surface, but when he looked behind to see Athena, there was nobody there but an echo of laughter in the trees.

He knelt and looked into the water and called out the names of Athena and Hiawatha, and wept. Somebody grasped his shoulder and again he looked behind to see who it was and he saw the woman working in the cafe standing beside the lake, bending over him with concern and warmth in her eyes.

For a moment Dylan couldn't place her, but then he realised that he was awakening and the cafe worker was really touching his shoulder gently and she was speaking to him.

"Are you alright child?" she asked softly, and Dylan smiled reassurance but felt the roughness in his throat that indicated he may have cried out in his sleep. He made a special effort to clear his head and to look clearly into the warm brown eyes of the woman who was worried for him. Her face was pleasantly, wrinkled, her earrings were long and ended in orange discs that hung so low they could brush her shoulders. Her eyelashes were long and curled, and her lipstick long worn away by the rigours of her night shift. She was smiling at him and there was a cup of steaming coffee she had just placed beside him. Dylan experienced a rush of gratitude which was written plainly on his face, which was all reassurance required for the kindly woman: so she patted his shoulder lightly and straightened up to stroll back behind the counter.

    The first light was just knocking the streetlights out as Dylan looked out of the window and realised that the problem of where to spend his first night was solved. He drank his coffee and thanked the woman who had let him sleep at the table all night, before walking back onto the street to do one more patrol of the street before venturing into the heart of the town to begin his search again.

Chapter Eighteen

Baxter had asked several questions of the strange fellow who had rescued him, but his words had just irritated the older man. He kept silent for as long as possible just following the man and doing what was indicated at the right time, until the silence pressed in upon him and he would break the silence with some inane observation and the older man would shake his head and glare from beneath his bushy brows.

They collected some wild garlic without words, not in silence because Baxter was still unable to move without grunting with effort, yelping in pain from leaning on a bramble or crunching twigs underfoot as if on purpose. Each time he made these noises, the other would pause and shake his head a little, as if disappointed or pained by the clumsy progress the youngster made through the wood, or indeed the world.

They stopped for some food, the canvas bag across the man's shoulder yielded up a few apples, and some nuts, which they ate sitting on a fallen log. The man seemed to be always looking at the surroundings as if it was signalling something to him, as he looked from Sky to woodland floor and then intently at a bush. Baxter wondered what he was seeing and eventually he started to say,

"I wish I could..." and tailed off his sentence knowing that the old man's opprobrium usually followed his attempts at conversation, but then they had usually been phatic statements, a light breath on the embers of an exchange designed to ignite a response and allow a conversation to conflagrate. He fell silent and stared at the ground.

"Well?" asked the quiet man.

Baxter looked at him amazed and open mouthed.

"What do you wish?" he persisted.

Baxter almost forgot what had been on his mind now that he was invited to say it, but he recovered the lost oar of his pondering and rowed the thought to shore.

"I wish I could be like... like you" he finished quietly.

"In what way?"

"You seem at home here and I wish I was" said Baxter feeling sorry for himself again and feeling foolish for speaking his feelings.

"Do ye really?" asked the older man, "Do ye really want to see what your place is in this world?"

"Yes" said Baxter with a defiant air

"Do ye trust me?"

Baxter faltered at that. He had trusted the man until now but this was different somehow and there was a hint of danger.

"Not really. Not yet" he admitted and the other threw back his head and barked a deep laugh.

"Good enow" he said slapping Baxter on the back. "Let's get ye a vision then" he said. Though Baxter was more confused than alarmed by this he still got up and followed the man through woodland until with a shock he realised they were back at the rough shelter without him even noticing that they had changed direction.

The older man poked about and pulled out little canvas bags from crevices here and there, something from a plastic storage crate, something from beneath his bedroll, while Baxter sat transfixed as a potion was mixed and heated on the stove in a pan, filtered and left to cool once brewed.

During this operation the older man had grinned conspiratorially at Baxter occasionally showing him a herb or a root with a wink as if Baxter should recognise the significance of the ingredient. At last the older man sat and let the potion stand and he turned to Baxter and said,

"If ye really want wisdom, understanding or whatever it is ye need, then it is here in this brew ye may find it if ye are strong enow. Are ye strong lad?"

Baxter felt the gravity of the offer and nodded seriously, and feeling ready for the test, if a test it was.

The odd fellow strained the brew through a rough cloth and the stringy collection of weeds and twigs it left behind looked like the contents of a waste bin after receiving the leavings of a cooked meal. He felt a little queasy at the thought, but still accepted the mug that was handed to him containing the filtered brew.

With one hand palm up lifted in a gesture which indicated he should drink, the man smiled and sat back as Dean Baxter took a chance and drank down the contents of the mug.

He downed it swiftly in case it was disgusting to taste but to his surprise it was nothing more than a lukewarm aromatic water, which sat easily on his stomach, and as the older man sat and whittled a spoon from a branch of pear tree with his impressive knife, Baxter relaxed and wondered if he had already passed the test. It was a good twenty minutes later that he noticed his teeth were itching, and for some reason that was mildly amusing. He ran his tongue over the tingling teeth and seemed to be able to feel every nerve in his mouth responding to the contact.

He glanced at his companion, who had sheathed his knife and was looking across at him with paternal concern.

"Relax lad, let it come" he said as Baxter sat back against the hay bale and took a deep breath. He saw the tent wall move, he saw the whole room mirror his breathing, then even the floor was moving in time with the rise and fall of his chest, but he was not concerned. It seemed natural that as he breathed, so the world moved in time with that, or was he breathing in time with the world? Yes that was it. He had found the rhythm of the world and was moving with it, and the man's hand on his shoulder was also moving in time with the breath of the world.

    He looked at the old man and saw he was older by the second, wrinkles and folds deepening in his face until he could only see a tissue of flesh stretched taught across the bones of his skull. Baxter screamed shrilly and tried to get up and run, but the skeletal figure was strong and pinned him down.

    In a deep slow voice it clacked its jaws and asked

    "What do ye see lad?"

    Baxter couldn't speak he was so terrified, he wanted to be outside where the air was cooler and the walls didn't seem to press in on him and no zombie man pinned him to the wall with his bony hand.

    "Outside!" was all he managed to say, and he pointed to the doorway with pleading eyes.

    The skeletal man held out his hand and lifted Baxter to his feet and supported him as he stepped out into the wood. On his hands and knees in the grass outside Baxter took great ragged breaths of the cool air and looked about him. There was smell in the air, something he could almost identify despite his senses seeming to be overdriven and spinning out of control stuffing his ears and eyes, nose and skin so full of sensation he could hardly bear it.

On the ground not far from where he was kneeling was the corpse of a bird, it was well rotted and maggots were there feasting and then he knew what he could smell. It was decay that assailed him. Everywhere about him, the man, the trees, the vegetation were all rotting, everything was dying, the world was dying, and he too must be dying. This was the truth of life, that everything is always dying, forever in a state of decay.

Again the old man asked him what he could see, and this time he was able to articulate it.

"Everything is dying, rotting, rotten" he barked at the ground in front of him as he gasped the air with its vegetable stench assaulting him with its impermanence and taunting his mortality.

Then he realised the man was talking to him softly and he tried to take in what he was saying.

"Good lad. Yes! But look deeper"

Baxter looked about him and could see only corpses of

trees, things that didn't know they were dying. How could he look deeper than the grave?

He looked at the tree again, at its scaly bark like a scab, at its long wilting branches and the bright green tips where buds were growing and something pricked his mind, something he had missed. Perhaps the old man was right, look deeper.

Again he looked at the corpse of the bird and saw the maggots cleaning up the body, he saw the grass growing around the little body, and suddenly he saw a dance. All about him the stench wasn't death, it was life after all, an endless succession of death and rebirth, he looked again at the man who had brought him here and in that face he saw the companion, the youth, the babe and the corpse all at once.

Baxter was unable to take it all in at once so he rolled onto his back and looked at the sky, and he saw the trees overhead and the clouds all whirling about in an endless dance of life, rebirth and never endingness that included the little soul of Dean Baxter who was invited to the dance if only he wanted to play.

Oh how he wanted to lay. He lay like that for a long time explaining what he saw, what he felt, what he KNEW to the approval of his guide.

Then they walked, and he found the ground was more a

part of himself than he had realised. The twigs and branches he could feel were just like him, reaching out to experience the world.

His guide pointed out this plant and that animal, showed him pathways where he had seen nothing before, pointed out where creatures hid or lived and when they finally approached the shelter again it was getting dark, but Dean still had too much to rearrange in his mind to be ready for sleep and the older man seemed resigned to sitting up with him through the night to talk and to listen as Dean's whole world was shuffled to accommodate this new and wonderful perspective he had gained.

When Dean awoke in the light of day and the inside of his mouth felt like the inside of his mouth had always felt, he was slightly disappointed. He looked at the trees and saw trees, but a gust of wind blew across the branches and the passage of the breeze moved along the bushes and ferns that lay in its path and once again the whole experience was his again and the life that throbbed through the Earth was tangible once more. He smiled and relaxed, because at this moment there was one thing he was certain about, he did not want his life to be the same again.

Clae

The fellow traveller who had given him the gift was fast asleep having spent his night looking after the young adventurer.

Dean set about trying to gather something to eat for when the other man awoke. It was with some surprise he found that if he didn't fight his way through the woodland he could move easily and relatively quietly through, and he noticed things that he had previously not seen. This was a strange new world for Dean and he thought he was going to like it.

Chapter Nineteen

In the library, the time was approaching when they would need to have some more light to continue. The oil lamp on a stand that Ballentine would allow would provide a little light but after some initial progress they had spent a long time reading the notes and journals of Fulmin Pinnock XII, they felt as though they were on the cusp of discovery but the hours had passed during which time a few calls had been made as a possible clue arose, or a reference to Brokken would appear in a margin note. The difficulty of the task was amplified by Pinnock's fascination with history so that a reference may be a casual one reflecting his passion, or a record of something he had found out, which was far more interesting but as yet, not terribly useful.

Burma was turning pages and scanning the text with greater accuracy and speed than her companions as she was far more accustomed to the written word despite the voracious reading habits of the others. So it was that she made good progress through the journals until she cried out in triumph.

"I have something!"

Athena and Apollo rushed to her side to see her discovery; Burma was pointing to the page, one finger extended in an accusatory fashion. Following the direction of the finger,

Athena read what she could see...

"...September 9th: I am very close to the secret now and feel sure that when I have symbols Interpreted I shall have the answer. The details are recorded in my Brokken Codex along with the drawings of the symbols."

Athena turned to Apollo.

"Apollo! Have you heard of the Brokken Codex?"

Apollo shook his head sadly.

"If it was here, on these shelves, I would have found it by now. I have looked so hard for books about him"

Both Athena and Burma knew this to be true but they needed to confirm that Ballentine had no other documents of books hidden away in other rooms.

Athena knew no fear of anybody as was appropriate for a nascent matriarch, so despite the lateness of the hour and Ballentine's uncharacteristic absence, she went quietly to the door of his inner sanctum and knocked sharply on the door. Behind the portal's heavy oak stopper, she heard an armchair creak as it yielded its sitting tenant, then soft footfalls approaching the door. The door opened and Mavis peered around it with a smile of greeting.

"We need Bally's help to find a codex" she explained.

"He's having a nap dear" Mavis explained "Can it wait for

tomorrow?"

Apollo took up the case and with a certain, ill concealed, zeal he explained,

"We think that Brokken had a secret power and it seems that The Emperor may have found it, nearly, but we can't find the book he wrote it in and maybe Ballentine has it!"

Mavis smiled at him impressed by such passion in one so young, but was about to protect Ballentine's rest with another rebuttal, when he appeared at her side, rubbing his head with hooded eyes and a stifled yawn.

"What are ye looking for?" he asked in his customary whisper.

Mavis put her hand out to him but he took the hand and held it tenderly, smiling at her with reassurance and gratitude.

"I am usually at hand for this work and often for far less interesting purpose than this grand quest"

His question had been rasped in the direction of Apollo, who repeated the summary he had given Mavis.

Ballentine nodded sagely throughout the explanation, then looking up to one side his eyes lost focus as he ran rapidly through his mental indexing system, then through the miscellany that resided in the drawers and in scroll cases stacked in a cupboard. As he drew his focus back to Apollo he was able to answer with confidence that no such item had he seen in the library.

The three explorers were crestfallen, having apparently got so close.

"What do we do next" asked Apollo, unaware of the finality of Ballentine's assertion. Burma laid a hand on his shoulder and shook her head sadly.

"I don't know" she told him "I really don't know"

Ballentine thought on for a moment, and then he suddenly raised a finger in a gesture which suggested an idea was forming and it needed a little more incubation before it was hatched. The others including Mavis, watched his face in wonder as his expression reflected the progress of the notion until with the onlookers holding their breath he finally dropped the finger to point it at Athena.

"Fulmin Pinnock was in the Black Coven, some say he was the head of the Coven for many years."

The wide eyed Apollo, made a slight squeak in the back of his throat at the mention of the Black Coven.

"It is late. I should be home" he said gathering up his papers and leaving almost at a run.

Burma looked a little frightened too at the mention of the feared Black Coven. Athena did not make a move as Ballentine's finger pointed at her, nor did she indicate by word or motion what she thought of the notion. She certainly didn't reveal the cold crawling sensation at the nape of her neck, and neither was she about to do so. She knew why Ballentine had pointed at her, it was because she alone of the group would dare consult the Black Coven in their meeting place, in the orchard, at night.

Burma realised too and seized Athena's arm.

"Oh no! Ye wouldn't go to the..." then with her voice dropping to the whisper worthy of Ballentine himself she finished "...Black Coven."

The defiant grin that fixed on Athena's face told Burma that she would indeed do just that unthinkable thing. Then Burma did something incredibly brave and selfless that surprised even herself.

"Then I shall go with ye"

Both Athena and Ballentine looked at the quiet, conservative Burma with a new respect and slight awe. Only Mavis had failed to grasp most of their meaning and none of their subtext.

Athena appreciated the gesture and in truth would have loved to take somebody with her. Somehow she felt certain that Dylan would have accompanied her and she would have been glad of his company, but Burma was not made for that type of escapade and Athena felt it would be an abuse of their friendship to accept the tremulous offer.

"Just one person needs to go my darling" she told Burma, "No use upsetting the Coven with crowds turning up there"

Burma felt that she should support Athena but there was a certain seductive logic to what she said, or was it just that she was so scared of the idea of facing the Coven that she would have accepted any argument that gave her an excuse to stay behind? If she went she would be terrified, but now she must stay and be terrified for Athena. Burma resigned herself to a sleepless night.

"Come to my house when ye return won't ye? I need to know ye are safe"

"Don't ye worry. I will be glad to share a bed with a comforting soul after my adventure in the orchard." Though she spoke in jest, there was no lack of feeling in what she said.

They wished Ballentine and Mavis a good night and Mavis waved them goodbye burning with curiosity that Ballentine would need to stay up late to satiate. Transmitting all he knew and all he had heard about the Black Coven.

At the willow tree on the crossroads, Burma said farewell to Athena and watched her walk past the brewery towards the orchards with her arms folded and a shiver that had little to do with the night chill. Athena was out of sight before Burma turned down the road heading south across the bridge over the dry bed of the River Henry to her father's cottage where she lived. No light shone from the window to indicate the William was at home, but he was probably already asleep. There was an unnatural quiet about the village with so much worry about the river.

Athena collected a lantern from the back of the brewery as she passed. It was one thing to go stamping about in the orchard at night, but it was quite another to do it without any light at all. The moonlight didn't penetrate the fruit trees well at this time of year, but at least they wouldn't be the bony fingers and skeletal arms that they became when winter stripped them of their verdant gowns.

As Athena made her way across the common, she was running through her head all the information she had heard about the Black Coven. Of course every person of status was rumoured to be a member and it was almost certain that the Bee Keeper was one of them, probably Daniel Dravot, the orchard manager, too. She found it difficult to imagine Uther as one of the secretive band of necromancers, but there were rumours.

At last she came to the orchard and moved as quietly as possible around the trees, looking and listening for a ritual fire or the sounds of chanting, anything to reveal the meeting place of the Black Coven. There was nothing at all to be seen or heard, and her relief was as sharp as her sense of anticlimax, the chance to meet the Black Coven had become an end in itself so she felt robbed of two goals.

She abandoned stealth and started to head back to the village square by the most direct route. This way took her near Brokken's Barrow, a long barrow on the fringe of the orchard and close to Collitt Semper's mustard crops. By skirting the edge of the fields she could avoid damaging the mustard and save time by avoiding going back through the orchard.

Brokken's Barrow was the name given to the long barrow but it was uncertain if Brokken had actually been responsible for it. There were stories told about this place too, such that folk tended to avoid it during the day, and more so at night. Of course this was Athena, who had so far had no contact with the barrow because she had never had reason to associate with it, except when she was younger and her childhood nemesis,

Clae

Virginia Wollstonecraft had challenged Athena to stand on top of the barrow on the Beltane evening. Of course Athena had done it and the challenge was returned. In fact it was Virginia's refusal to stand atop the barrow as Athena had done that broke her hold on Athena. In truth Virginia had watched Athena with her fists on her hips, feet apart and her long dark hair whipped by the wind on the barrow and felt quite frightened of her presence and courage.

Now as Athena passed close by she recalled these incidents and smiled to herself and then she heard a noise like a deep rumbling laugh. Unable to dismiss such things and considering the possibility that she may yet discover the Black Coven's whereabouts, she paused and cocked her head to the breeze in the hope of catching more sounds and a direction.

Sure enough, there it was again, a guttural laugh, and it seemed to come from the direction of the long barrow. Holding the lantern in front of her more as a talisman than a guide, she made her way around the foot of the barrow to the stones that marked its old entrance, long boarded up and covered with creeper vines some of which turned blood red in the autumn.

The sounds were coming from behind the panel and she crept closer to better hear what it was possible to catch.

It sounded to Athena as if they were counting souls, or

body parts, and she shuddered despite herself and wondered if this was the Black Coven, would they allow her to return to the village or would she too become something to be counted.

She distinctly heard that count and somebody had said "Two for his heels" she also heard a reference to "good hands" and another voice said somebody had "pegged out" which in Clae was an irreverent euphemism for death.

With so much fear building up inside her, Athena had to stop and take stock for a moment, gathering her wits, mastering her panic, forcing down the excitement that threatened to engulf her, and face her fear.

Once she was breathing regularly again, even though her heartbeat was like the mechanism of the brewery clock thumping in her chest, she stepped up to the boarding and felt around it for an opening. Sure enough, to one side, at the very bottom, was a crawl space covered with vegetation and a separate loose board.

Moving the loose board to one side she was able to squat down and look inside which was possible because it was lit by a lantern. There were people there but her view was obscured by her angle and the person sitting with their back closest to the entrance.

She crawled forward with her own lamp before her, and

suddenly every person in the barrow was aware that an interloper was among them. They all stood and faced the newcomer so that when Athena stood up she could see every face in the place.

Daniel Dravot, the orchard manager; Shylock Giza, the miller; Ben Caliban, the Brewery engineer, Danube Munich who had been a childhood friend and other familiar faces peered at her with interest, even Frank Curiosity was intrigued, but nobody spoke.

In the silence Athena looked at the table and saw a bottle of Mustik and some earthenware cups, a deck of playing cards, well used, and a wooden board with holes all the way along its rectangular length. What was the significance of the holes and the markers that sat beside the board?

Frank Curiosity whose laugh she had heard was the first break the silence. In the deepest, most impressive baritone he could muster after assaulting his vocal chords with Mustik he boomed,

"What do ye want of the Black Coven?" at which the whole assembly dissolved into tipsy laughter.

"Is this really the black coven?" she asked feeling rather let down and a little cross that she had been terrified by this rather unfrightning group of gentlemen, many of whom she was very fond and had no idea that they would be mixed up in something diabolical like the Coven.

Ben Caliban nodded and pulled up a log for her to sit upon as he saw she must have screwed up a great deal of valour to make this visit. Athena accepted the seat gratefully and the others resumed their seats too once she had settled.

"What is this?" asked Athena looking at the table and its contents.

"A game, called Cribbage" explained Shylock. "It has been played here for generations, but in secret to keep the legend of the Black Coven alive"

"But why?" Athena had to ask.

"Well it gets us out of the house and it's a good game" explained Frank.

"No! I meant why keep the legend of the Black Coven alive at all"

"Well you would have to ask Uther I suppose, but it has to do with people being a little bit frightened, it does 'em some good to have something real to be scared by. It also means there is something looking out for them in a way."

The game was apparently at a convenient point to pause, though it was all but forgotten in the light of this visit. Athena had more questions though.

"Who knows about this?"

"Well Uther knows obviously, Frank just blabbed that" said Ben, shooting a narrow eyed glance at a sheepish Frank Curiosity. "The last person to come here with a question is the only other person who knows"

"Who was that?" she asked half expecting to have this question rejected, after all they had told her much and she expected the limit to be imposed quite soon.

"The only other person to seek us out was Desdemona when she was about your age"

Athena smiled with pride that she had followed in the footsteps of the one person in Clae whose footsteps she hoped to be worthy to follow.

"Can you help me?" she said at last.

"Maybe we can help each other" said Ben, "What is it ye need?"

"I'm trying to find the Brokken Codex written by Emperor Fulmin Pinnock"

At this Danube Munich spoke up, but hesitantly being the youngest of the assembly and newly initiated into the Black Coven.

"I may have an idea where to look" and all eyes turned toward him with interest.

"Please don't tell Burma about this will you?" he asked looking about the room and back to Athena. A ribald jeer went around the room and ended in a hiccough from Danube, who was very interested in Burma but rather too unsure of himself to let her know, though the whole village knew and Burma was patiently waiting to see if he was ever going to mention it.

Athena saw there was no value in revealing the Black Coven's true nature and made a solemn oath to protect their secrecy as Desdemona had done before her.

Danube then described an incident when he was younger and studying his letters in the library, when his pet mouse had escaped. He had been mortified and little terrified at the prospect of a rodent loose amongst all of those manuscripts so he had devoted his spare time to tracking it down when everyone else had returned to their work in the afternoon. Whilst cornering the mouse and just prior to recapturing it, he had found a small hole at the back of one of the shelves when he removed the books. It was too small fro his mouse but big enough for a finger to be inserted and inside he had felt a spring. He had imagined that it could be a hidden panel for more shelves or such but had been too timid to attempt finding out.

Armed with detailed information about how to find the

shelf and the hole, Athena thanked the friendly group and went on her way smiling to herself as she trudged homeward, planning a good yarn to spin for Burma that was neither too far from believable or an outright lie; after all the legend could do with a little extra spice now and again, just to keep it lively and give it some zest.

Chapter Twenty

When Hiawatha awoke in the shed he was unsure if it was yet light but filtered by the greasy window pane or if it was sill the middle of the illuminated night. When he stood and looked from the window it was apparent that both were partly true, the sunrise was underway but the street lights had yet to switch off, and as Hiawatha looked out at the limited view that the window and its veil of filth offered of the outside world, he was aware of the street lights snapping off one by one, which was in itself a wonder to him despite his aversion to the unsettling effect their light had upon him.

Before long he was thinking of moving along, and wondering if he should go before placing George, his host, in a difficult position should Hiawatha be discovered having an illicit nap in the shed, or to stay until George told him it was safe to leave. It went against the grain to sneak anywhere and to leave like a thief in the night seemed somehow to render cheap, the generosity of the offer of shelter.

Hiawatha settled to think and wait and occupy himself as he might, until the day was properly established before leaving to give George every opportunity to see his guest leave and to be thanked for his kind gesture. The next ninety minutes were spent listening to the unfamiliar sounds of a town awakening with the backing vocals of familiar birdsong.

Eventually the door opened gently, if not quietly, and George poked his head cheerfully around the door and seeing Hiawatha awake and sitting up, grinned and asked.

"Did you sleep alright in there?"

"Yes! Thank ye" Hiawatha replied with a matching smile.

"Well the coast is clear, and the olds have cleared of to the office, so you can come and grab some breakfast if you fancy"

Most of the sentence was lost on Hiawatha but he knew what breakfast meant and he was quite glad to accept the offer.

George suddenly seemed to see the shed for the first time and realised how Hiawatha had occupied himself. All the junk that had been tossed into the shed was stacked and arranged as neatly as possible, a broom had been found and employed to reveal the floorboards and make a substantial pile of sweepings by the door. Loose nails had been collected into empty jars and tins and the metal shelving had been cleared, bent back into shape and reloaded with a tidier arrangement.

Stepping into the shed and looking about George chuckled and swore gently.

"You've been busy" he said needlessly, as Hiawatha squatted down to sweep the pile of dust into a dustpan and empty it outside the shed door.

"That is definitely worth a good breakfast. I should score some merit points with the olds if I claim responsibility later. C'mon let's get some grub"

He looked round the shed one more time shaking his head in amused wonder before laying a friendly hand on Hiawatha's shoulder and guiding him to the back door, into the kitchen, where he had been preparing to make toast.

As a couple of thick slices emerged from under the grill and were slathered in butter, the two sat at the table and passed the time in conversation.

"That was a really good laugh last night" George informed Hiawatha, in case he had forgotten. Hiawatha made no immediate answer as he was struggling with trying to swallow the bread. He found the texture very doughy and sticky, but he did not wish to offend. He nodded in lieu of a vocal response.

"Where are you from then, with your strange accent"

Hiawatha was mindful of Dylan's warning about keeping safe the secret of Clae's existence, but he was also quite revolted at the idea of lying, so he made his answer as vague as possible.

"Not far from here really" he explained, but George was

not convinced;

"Nobody round here talks like you though" George persisted. Hiawatha now felt a little cornered and was flailing for a plausible and truthful misdirection.

"Near Treaton" he said.

"Ah, I see" George replied with a mischievous grin, "You're a carrot cruncher. Now it makes sense"

Hiawatha was puzzled by this, but he saw that George was satisfied with his explanation and also assumed that he liked carrots apparently. He concluded that the carrots were a lucky guess but said nothing more about it. Instead he directed the conversation back the other way.

"Where are ye from?" he asked. George looked a little startled at the question.

"With this accent?" he said "I was born and raised in this dump". Hiawatha was unsure how the last comment had been meant, so he thought it best to drop the subject and move along to safer topics.

"Thank ye for the place to sleep" he said, and George smiled again as he got up to toast another two slices of bread under the grill.

"No problem – Happy to help" he assured his guest. "Where are you going to sleep tonight?" he asked effectively affirming that the accommodation had been a single night only, which Hiawatha had already assumed and expected. He remembered the address in the bottom of his bag and patting the bag he said

"I have an address to visit" more to reassure George but it had reminded him that he did in fact have that option. George seemed pleased too.

"What are you going to do about money?" George enquired, but when Hiawatha made no response, fearing that revealing his ignorance was unwise, George assumed it was pride that prompted the silence, and pursued it no further.

After the meal George and Hiawatha parted company and Hiawatha again expressed his thanks for the food and shelter. George was happy to have obliged, and felt a certain noblesse oblige that falls upon the shoulders of those with, to protect those without. It seems to be that the young are more awake to this than their elders. To George, the luxury of a house in which to live, gave him responsibilities to a homeless person he chanced upon on the street.

George watched Hiawatha as he walked steady and relaxed, off down the street in search of this address he had written on a piece of paper. He liked what he knew of Hiawatha, a daft name, a really uninhibited way of dancing, a great laugh, a brilliant shed cleaner and organiser. Perhaps he was a little odd though.

George turned to go back into the house but looked over his shoulder to see the last glimpse of his guest as he rounded the bend at the end of the road.

"We are all freaks!" he said to himself as he went inside and shut the door.

Now the rain had passed, the population was out of doors, so as Hiawatha found his way back to the High Street, it was thronged with shoppers and the noise was beyond a joke. Hiawatha caught his breath at the volume of chatter, cars and trucks rumbling along the road, stopping at the lights to foul the air a little more before rumbling on. A police car warbled and screeched past the traffic and Hiawatha had to clamp his hands to his ears to protect himself from the discomfort of the volume and pitch. Traffic crossing signals beeped and people talked into something they held to the side of their head, talking as if they were having a conversation with an unseen companion. They didn't seem to be more than vaguely aware of where they were and what they were doing. It alarmed and unnerved Hiawatha, it seemed so inhuman and peculiar.

His route led past an old Coaching Inn with a wide gate

into a courtyard where travellers had once stopped for rest on their journey to and from the nearest major towns and cities. This was once a market town and was place of semi-respectable accommodation in the days of the turnpike roads. The Inn was now converted to an indoor emporium with the cobbled courtyard preserved as a curiosity in a rapidly changing town.

    Across the arch of the entrance was a sign which advertised the market within. When Hiawatha saw the sign he was reminded of the familiar warmth of the traditional Clae market, the friendliness and bustle. He was attracted by that memory so he went to the gates and was moved along involuntarily by the throng coming and going, so he found himself inside without quite being sure if he now wanted to be inside at all such was the crowd. People were enjoying what they considered to be a civilised degree of personal space about themselves but it seemed to Hiawatha to be intrusive to the point of intimate. He found it impossible to back away to a comfortable distance without backing into somebody else who considered being stepped on as uncomfortably close.

    It was a few frantic minutes before he grew accustomed to the discomfort and could relax sufficiently to navigate to a safe harbour against a wall where a wooden trellis allowed wisteria to clamber the wall and cascade like a cataract over the upstairs windows.

      Standing to one side and watching the crowds he was able to observe the customs and peculiarities of this community in its meeting place. The first thing he noticed was the lack of familiarity. Nobody greeted anybody by name or with a smile that made it far from their lips and never got as far as the eyes. Occasionally a vague familiarity may be evident in the interactions between a trader a regular customer, but the greetings were superficial, shallow and cool like a dew pond on a spring morning.

      Robbed of even the displaced familiarity of other people he fell to watching the transactions and noting what changed hands. There was no barter at all. The traders all took only notes and coins while the people passing through took only the goods and often without much apparent interest in what they were accepting. They barely examined the goods, they exchanged no gratitude other than the empty 'thank you' that was passed back and forth like a soft apple that nobody wanted to keep hold of.

      He noted the variety of clothing, colours and styles, he noted the ages of the folk coming and going were very old or very young, there seemed to be nobody his own age about at all. He saw that the people were mostly strangers to one another and when people did seem to be friends they arrived together and left together. Very occasionally he saw two people stop and chat with familiar ease, but in such a setting it seemed odd to him and vaguely disturbing to see a caricature of friendship in such an impersonal setting.

    Seeing and inhaling the aroma of food he was starting to wonder when his breakfast would manage to be digested to the point he could seriously contemplate eating something and hard on the heels of that thought came the realisation that he had no means of acquiring food as he had nothing to exchange.

    Tiring of the constant flow of people and the ceaseless unsmiling thanks that were chanted throughout each sale, he mustered his courage and plunged through the arch to emerge breathless and perspiring on the street again. Looking about he was lost for a clue about where to go. More than a few of Dylan's warnings were haunting him at this point and he was beginning to realise that this adventure was one for which he was singularly ill equipped. Such knowledge as might have served him well, was unavailable to him in Clae and seemed wholly unappealing at this stage. Pulling himself together he decided to see if he could find something to redeem this adventure and make sense of this place.

    Once more he set off along the pavement, following the

Clae

signs to the Market Square in case that was something more recognisable to him than the chaotic bazaar he had just escaped.

Chapter Twenty one

The dawn broke without Burma or Athena seeing it arrive; this was unusual, for both were early risers and a worried excitement was frothing through the community in exactly the same way as the River Henry had frothed at the Sluice of the Mill until its recent profane desiccation.

The reason that the two women slept as the village fretted, was the nocturnal adventure and its draining effect upon them both. Though the sun had risen, they slept on, Burma still clinging to her friend in fright and grateful relief at her safe return.

It was mid morning before Athena led the way to the Manor House to be greeted softly by Ballentine and Mavis, arms linked, as they welcomed the visitors. Athena wasted no time as she headed to the library leaving the others gently bobbing in her wake, as Burma explained the latest development to them both.

By the time the story was told and they made their way into the library, Athena had carefully removed the books from the lower shelf and stacked them, neatly and in order, on a nearby table of burr elm with an inlaid geometric marquetry design with a distinct Art Deco flavour and a highly polished lacquer finish.

Ballentine allowed himself only the briefest of frowns at the displaced books and the use of the table before devoting his attention to Athena as she crouched close to the floor and reached out with a tentative finger to prod at the mechanism behind the shelf.

Puzzled disappointment was shared among the group as nothing whatsoever happened. Athena, extended a forefinger and cast a meaningful glance at the others as once more she headed for the orifice. All hesitation was irrelevant as she stabbed at whatever lay behind the wood with an impatient thrust of a rigid digit and was rewarded almost instantly by a loud metallic echoing click from the wall.

The tension was like a fog in the air of the library as each froze in expectation of something more about to happen, but as the silence remained intact a certain disappointment descended as first one, then another began to shift position, or to cough softly until defeat permeated the mood.

Ballentine experimentally pushed and pulled the shelf to see if a secret compartment should reveal itself, but the shelf seemed as solid as before, perhaps more so in the face of the hope and expectation they had allowed.

Mavis however had long read Agatha Christie, Edgar Allen Poe and such, so she looked nearby to see what else may have changed. It was her sharp eyes and wit that detected the adjacent shelving was standing slightly proud, so she gripped the front edge of the shelf and pulled it experimentally and then with more force until it emitted a shriek of such pitch and ferocity that everybody, including Mavis recoiled in horror; partly because the noise had been an unearthly approximation of a human cry of pain, though in a moment they all realised that it had been metal on rusty metal that had produced the cry.

Athena and Ballentine lent their assistance to the task and a further tortured screech was elicited from the mechanism before a the shelf pivoted on its vertical axis with half the shelf protruding into the room and half recessed into the wall leaving a small opening accessible between the shelves and a dark space visible beyond, but only just. The space appeared to be sufficient to allow the passage of a slender framed individual moving crabwise in the darkness and the corridor led to who knew where?

While the Clae natives were still agog at the revealed passage, Mavis was trying to squeeze herself into it. Ballentine clasped her arm in alarm, entreating her to stay in the Library.

"Nobody has been in there for decades" he warned, but Mavis shook her head smiling. Laying a gentle hand on his forearm she explained.

"Books don't really talk, Bally dear. That voice I heard came from here"

Ballentine beamed at her with admiration but did not release her to explore. It was Athena who made it clear who the explorer would be, as she was as slender as Ballentine but not so tall and far more courageous than Burma.

Ballentine fetched the oil lamp and lit it for her, in order that she may see her way and discover what may be there to help them in their quest.

Athena squeezed into the opening, placed the lamp on the floor and like a rehearsing mime artist, palms flat against the wall, she shuffled sideways along the passage. It followed the wall but sloped down until after a subjectively interminable trek she reached a solid wall, and enough space to turn around; some dry leaves and twigs crunched crisply underfoot. Having moved beyond the range of the lamp she was again in near darkness and shuddered as her imagination painted pictures on the black canvas before her eyes.

The three walls were solid brick, no mechanism, no door, no way out, no answers and no news with which to return. As she cast her eyes about one last time she saw a flash of sunlight on her hand. No more than a sliver had caught her skin and reflected but she moved about until she held that slender ray of hope on her hand and traced it back to the roof of the tiny room. Up there was a splinter of daylight sneaking in through a crack in the roof.

Athena now focussed on what may be above her, reaching up to feel the brickwork and discovering a handhold, then another. Looking down she detected the deeper dark that told of similar footholds and using these evenly spaced crannies, she quickly scaled the wall to press against the roof which revealed itself to be a heavy wooden door which allowed some movement but resisted opening with a jangle that suggested a hasp outside which had been closed and pinned.

Intrigued but ultimately thwarted, Athena climbed back down and felt her way back to the light of the lamp and to the waiting welcome of friendly faces, but as she got to the opening her eyes were making more use of the available light and saw something on the wall which could not be accessed unless the door was closed with her on the inside. No matter how hard Athena strained to see past the part of the shelf that had moved inward to obstruct the passageway she could not see the object of her attention.

"There is something on the wall up ahead. Close the door to let me see it"

"No child" was Bally's whispered response, "Come out now, where it is safe"

Athena had not spent time with Desdemona for nothing, so the tone with which she demanded the closing of the door brooked no dissent, and though she inwardly quaked at the prospect, she herself helped them from the other side as they heaved against the reluctance of the shelf to close and to seal her inside.

Without bothering to shut the entrance securely she was able to pass the obstruction and see the object for what it was by the light of the lamp, now that it was no longer casting a heavy shadow over the area of interest. When she was close enough to see it, Athena could see it was a brass plate, which had been engraved, apparently freehand by an amateur with some artistic ability. Despite the light it was too dark to clearly see what was depicted.

Huffing with effort and frustration, Athena shuffled back to the opening and called through for thin paper and charcoal, the usual writing paper made in Clae being too heavy for a successful rubbing image to be collected. After waiting in the passage with her back on one wall and knees against the other, for a time that seemed to drag by with particular indolence which was honed by the discomfort, until the creak of the mechanism allowed Burma's hand to flourish the rewards of their search.

Athena took the rubbing and passed It back for inspection. As soon as Ballentine declared it legible, she stepped aside as the exit was pushed into view to allow Athena and the lamp to escape the dreary hole.

Everything was soon restored to its rightful place and the image could now be examined at leisure. It appeared to be a drawing of a part of the Manor House and an inscription which read "Vita Briton Brokka".

"I don't think that is correct Latin" observed Mavis, but only Ballentine took any notice and acknowledged her contribution with a smile and a gentle squeeze of her hand.

"I wonder what it means?" said Athena expecting the book knowledge of her companions to provide an answer. She was not disappointed as Mavis provided part of the answer;

"Vita means life and Briton refers to the old inhabitants of England"

Ballentine breathed the last part of the puzzle as he had seen references to Brokken, the semi-legendary founder of the village, where he had been recorded as Brokka; in the personal papers of Emperor Fulmin Pinnock XII.

With a satisfactory explanation provided and a feeling

that a clue was in their grasp, the quartet were addressing the image when the door opened and Apollo strolled in with his usual equipment. Excited by the possibility of a new chapter in the adventure opening up he rushed over to see what was soaking up the attention of the others.

It appeared to be a strange face, slightly askew, and a small cruciform at its base, the word 'Sinister" was scratched beside it twice, and as the wave of hope began to break on the barren shores of despair, the crest had not yet fallen when Apollo squeaked his recognition.

"It's the corner man" he said by way of explanation but nobody was any the wiser.

Pointing to the corner of the library where he retreated, the least travelled corner of the large room, he indicated the beams and again proclaimed it to be the corner man.

Mystified, the group followed him to the quiet space where he habitually sat, and he wordlessly pointed up, but again there was no response from the others. Standing with his back to the chimney breast and indicating up and to the right of the ceiling beam it was now possible for the others to make out a carving in the corner between wall, beam and chimney, a green man with a vine trailing from his mouth from which grew leaves framing his head with an aura of flora.

Ballentine was fetching his wooden stepladder when Apollo asked.

"Why does it say sinister? He looks friendly to me, he's smiling anyway."

Mavis nodded in agreement and made a suggestion,

"Sinister can mean 'left' too"

"But it's on the right of the chimney" protested the young man.

"Not if you are facing the room" Burma pointed out. Athena was already crossing to the other side of the hearth and trying to peer up where the space was obscured further by a tall bookcase, but craning her neck she saw the outline of a matching figure on the beam.

"I think ye are a clever lad" she told a beaming Apollo.

Ballentine brought the ladder to where Athena now stood and once again it was her duty to explore while others watched. She climbed the ladder and looking briefly and apologetically at Ballentine placed one foot on an upper shelf to better look at the carving.

"Sinister, Sinister" reminded Mavis as Athena reached out and so with an extended arm she turned the figure left to resemble the scratched image, and as it turned it revealed the cruciform carved into the wood. A dull thump sounded the other side of the chimney where the figure's twin was found.

Athena descended as the others cautiously investigated the noise. On the far side of the hearth a wooden panelled wall had opened up its panel to reveal a priest hole. Even Mavis was confused about why a Manor House as isolated as this one and in any event to be unlikely to have any involvement in the ebb and flow of religious power, should have a priest hole, complete with religious insignia and pre-Christian images. There was no time to contemplate further as Apollo was carefully opening the panel to reveal a wooden trunk with ornate hinges, fastened with a hasp and staple with a locking pin.

Ballentine lifted it out and placed it on the floor. Everybody crowded in as he withdrew the pin and lifted the latch. The lid was raised and there inside was a neatly stacked pile of small books and documents, on the top of the pile was a smartly bound volume of hand written notes in careful copperplate, entitled "An investigation into the life of the Ancient Briton named Brokken, the father of Clae – The result of study by Fulmin Pinnock XII of the Clae Empire"

The notes inside were neatly written but not as ornate as the hand in which the title was recorded.

Apollo was almost weeping with excitement and joy as they all leaned in to listen as Burma began to read.

Clae

Chapter Twenty Two

Mathias Woodbine, the seer and mystic had long since taken to living the life of a hermit in the uncut fringe of Clae, where he lived a half life of the semi outlaw; Not able to comfortably walk through the village but not friendless either, as he enjoyed the irregular company of a few of the less socially active members of the community. Daniel Dravot the orchard manager and The beekeeper liked him for his ability to live alone as they did. He was also able to trade some interesting goods with these fine folk, to keep him in a certain level of comfort in his hidden tent, and to supply Clae with occasional items he was able to bring in from the outside.

Today was a fresh start, cleaned by heavy rain and still smelling damp and green. A new perspective had been introduced to Dean Baxter and the gunsel had found his horizons broadened as his adventures had opened his doors of perception and kept a foot in the way to stop him closing them again in fright. Now was time to show the boy what life in Clae was like behind the scenes, away from the bustling village square.

A light breakfast had been prepared when Mathias awoke, and he smiled approval at Dean for his efforts. Smiling was something not entirely easy for Mathias Woodbine and yet he had done more than usual in the last couple of days.

When they had finished their meal, Mathias packed away the equipment and hid the dwelling from the eyes of passers-by, should there be any. He started off through the woodland with Dean at his heels making less noise than before, he noted approvingly and not fighting his own body and the environment, relaxing and concentrating on what he was doing, instead of wondering why everything was against him. In this way he was seeing the briar before it snagged him, and sliding his foot to rest instead of crunching whatever was beneath his boot. In this fashion they covered quite a distance without complaint or incident, Dean increasing in confidence and enjoyment with every time that Mathias pointed out some creature's track, trail, burrow nest or hiding place or the creatures themselves, often close enough that he could reach and touch them if he chose to, but he did not.

At last they emerged from the wild woodland into a managed woodland thick with fruit trees. Mathias moved this way and that until they reached a tiny cabin, outside of which sat the Orchard Manager, Daniel Dravot, on a log and carving a wooden spoon from an apple branch using a very well used knife with a pear handle and a six inch blade. There was a lazy expertise to his movements as if this was something he did often and knew the shape and eventual form of the spoon that was emerging from the wood, as if he had known it before he had first touched the blade to the timber; that the design stage had been to look at the branch until the spoon it contained had suggested itself to Daniel, and only then had be begun to whittle.

Although he was aware of the visitors, he did not look up from his work or utter any greeting. Mathias seemed in no hurry to announce himself indicating that Dean should sit and took position beside Daniel on the log without a sound.

After some time, the bowl and handle of the spoon became obvious but not clearly defined, the work suddenly ceased and Daniel regarded Dean with something akin to suspicion. Dean leaned forward and rose slightly extending his hand to shake the hand of this stranger and opened his mouth to make an overture of friendly greeting.

"Hsst!" said Daniel waving at Dean to be silent. Blushing with embarrassment Dean resumed his seat. A protracted silence was broken by nothing at all; not even the sound of Dean shifting his weight from one buttock to the other to relieve the creeping numbness beginning to deaden his nether regions and spreading towards his groin. He dared not move and risk further censure from Daniel.

Daniel eyed him suspiciously throughout and eventually pointed his knife at him and asked,

"Are ye wise?"

Dean shook his head, still too intimidated to speak.

"Then listen to the wise one" advised Daniel. But as Dean leaned in with a pantomime of attention to Daniel's every word, Daniel laid the knife gently on the log beside him and stared back at Dean. This charade continued for a few moments before Daniel addressed Mathias and simply said, "Tell him"

Mathias sat beside Dean and sighed.

"Ye remember the night ye saw something?" Dean nodded slowly recalling the feeling and images. "Ye saw life, nature, the world". Dean nodded again as he felt again the way he had been part of everything he could sense about him.

The look in his eyes satisfied Mathias enough to continue.

"That was the wise one speaking to ye" he explained.

Dean began to see what they were getting at and nodded again.

"If ye chatter like a bird, ye will not hear the wise one speak to ye, and even birds have more to say than ye do." Placing one rough hand on Dean's hair and playfully cuffing the lad about the head he added, "The birds are prettier than ye as well."

Daniel shook his head at all this chatter but Mathias ignored him and chuckled at his own joke, until even Dean had to smile. Daniel picked up his knife and standing up he melted away into the woodland to better hear the wise one and let the fools make noise. All the same, he was considering introducing the lad to The Beekeeper, he should get on with the bees, he thought, they were noisy buggers too.

Dean had found the situation vaguely embarrassing, but not particularly vexatious to his mind or spirit. In fact the skills he was acquiring were those he had practiced with his Uncle Norman, the same person who had taken him camping and spent days fishing in silence, feeling safe from having to speak and feeling foolish when his words betrayed him by conveying a different message from that which he had intended.

The feeling of safety, the feeling of belonging was returning to him, without the menace of the guns, or the implied threat. Mathias was guiding him home and he would follow that pathfinder into the next world if it would continue to provide him with the sense of complete satisfaction that kept bathing him in its unfamiliar and almost forgotten warmth.

The Beekeeper was not at home, but they sat for a companionable hour outside his lodge where his frames were being constructed, before moving quietly off along a woodland track to the next point of interest.

The intermittent sun was confounded by the woodland as it struggled to warm the tough hide of Mathias Woodbine and his companion. Dean no longer gave any thought to their destination or purpose as he settled into the pace set by Mathias and followed unquestioning wherever the path took them.

Had that path taken them to the door of the local constabulary, Dean would have followed; unwilling to the last to accept that the man he followed could mean him harm.

The brief sunshine flickered between the leafy boughs with stroboscopic urgency and yet the day trickled past as leisurely as the last dregs of the River Henry; a mere trickle in its paucity of splash.

About the time Dean became aware that his leader was slowing the pace, he noticed too, a change in the flora. Scratching, piercing, stinging plants grew in abundance and old gnarled alder trees hampered progress by huddling together to warm each other where their sylvan overcoats were thinly inadequate but the topmost branches of larch wove a canopy that succeeded in deflecting most of the available sunlight. The ground was boggy underfoot and where a foot was placed it had to be lifted again with effort and with a slurping sound as it lifted free of the thick mud.

Eventually the duo broke through into a clearing where a lean-to shelter was slouching against the base of a rock face that rose about eight metres above its slate roof. The structure looked as though it could comfortably house two people sitting down but little more than that. A well made wooden door and a shuttered window occupied most of the available space in that wall, the roof sloped up from the front to the rock above: though the window shutters were open, the angle of approach was such that Dean could see nothing within.

Mathias stamped his feet as if dislodging the dust from his boots, but Dean realised he was announcing his arrival and almost immediately a figure appeared at the window and a woman's voice cried out "Woody!"

The woman flung the door open and herself into the arms of Mathias Woodbine. Even with her arms wrapped about his head, Dean could see the rosy glow rising from his collar to bloom on Woodbine's cheeks. Dean realised he was bashful or being starved of air, but went with the former suggestion and averted his eyes for a moment until the greeting had lowered in its intensity. The woman, still clasping Woodbine's forearms held him at arm's length to assess him and grin. It was only then that she noticed Dean and asked.

"Who are ye my handsome fellow?"

This time it was Dean who blushed, but did not know how to answer: could not answer, because she had turned her face to him and the power of speech had abandoned him and left him fumbling and awkward again.

Her close cropped golden hair framed her rounded cheeks like feathers; the green of her eyes though flecked with grey, shone in the sunlight. Each of these features alone could be described as pleasant; even together they could prompt some to employ an adjective such as 'pretty': however, in this woman were arranged in such proportions to create such an effect that the only explanation that made sense and justified the existence of the world and all its creatures, was that written on the face of this woman was a faithful representation of her personality, her generosity of spirit, kindness, love of all living creatures and her boundless, constant joy in sharing the world with the everyday, which every day amazed her.

Half remembered or perhaps not quite forgotten fairytales, insinuated their ghosts into his vision, as he admired this princess in her forest isolation; had seven dwarves emerged from the woodland calling greetings he would have remained unsurprised, but so unexpected was the sight of this beautiful woman, he could but stare.

Fortunately Woodbine was swift with introductions.

"This be my little Weasel" he told her cuffing Dean lightly to help him regain his dignity and allow the woman some in return. To Dean he said,

"This be Mrs Catchamole"

She huffed in mock despair at this private joke and corrected him.

"My name is Baba Yaga" then widening her eyes she added laughing "I have a witch's name".

Dean looked at Mathias who nodded seriously to confirm the truth of that statement.

It was much later that Dean appreciated the significance of her short hair, when he recalled that the women of Clae wore long hair, sometimes restrained with ribbon or bun, but not cut. This was another mark of her difference; the full effect of which he had only had the vaguest scent.

What he had failed to appreciate was that her rejection of her hair was an aspect of her rejecting her great beauty and even the society of the villagers as she despaired at being considered in terms of her appearance alone and sought refuge in the isolation of her life away from the daily society of Clae to better enjoy and savour the rare contact she had with others beyond those with whom she shared the isolation.

"Come inside" she offered, extending an arm towards the open door. Dean looked doubtfully at the lean-to shack but Mathias propelled him onward with a hand on his shoulder and in this fashion he crossed the threshold and discovered that the wooden facade concealed an excavated accommodation in the hillside, which proved to be spacious and airy. As Baba Yaga came into the room she went to the back wall where a bell was hanging. Nearby a rope disappeared into the rock and as she approached she gave two short tugs on the rope before busying herself at the fireside making a hot infusion to share with her guests.

As she busied herself she exchanged news and gossip with Mathias, but none of it concerned people known to Dean, so he held his peace and looked admiringly at Baba Yaga without being too obvious.

Five steaming cups were soon prepared and Dean looked about to see a clue as to the identity of the intended recipients of the extra drinks. Mathias paid no attention to the drinks and Baba Yaga offered none to either guest. A short while later the door opened and Baba Yaga jumped to her feet and said

"Here they are at last"

A huge filthy man stood in the doorway, silhouetted

against the light from outside. His shoulders rounded forward and his head looked flat. He stepped into the room and nodded at Woodbine.

"Mathias"

"Little Mole" replied Mathias.

Incredulity prompted Dean to break his silence.

"Little Mole" he echoed, failing to keep a note of amused wonder from his tone.

Baba Yaga stepped in to explain.

"Little Mole was prenticed to Old Mole so he was called Little Mole."

"I were little when I were prenticed" said Little Mole. "My prentice is just called Mole though"

By this time Dean had been able to take in the features of Little Mole, the flat forehead that hung like a mantel over his deep set eyes, slate grey, with burninig embers within; flat nose, thin lips, loose soil in his hair and dirt ground in to the skin so firmly it was like a pigment. This was not a man possessed of great looks and yet Baba Yaga clasped his arm and rested her head on his shoulder as if he was a film star and she his attendant admirer, and he responded with no less affection.

The door again swung open and in came another that

had to be the apprentice mentioned a moment ago; this must be Mole.

Though similarly filthy he and Little Mole were of a different build; Mole being slighter and not so tall. But as he crossed the room, he assumed a seat facing the window, so it was only as he sat that he was clearly visible to the visitors, Dean was shocked by his appearance.

The lower jaw was the focus of Dean's attention as it protruded, or intruded, further than even his hooked nose. His lower lip seemed to be unable to cover his bottom teeth which gleamed like polished marble against the swarthy ochre of his grime ingrained cheeks.

Dean made and maintained eye contact carefully with Mole to avoid staring at his more obvious attributes. Moles attention swung to Dean and fixed him with an appraising look as light and subtle as a cold chisel.

Dean, with effort, kept his attention fixed with on Mole's eyes and Mole seemed satisfied when Dean hesitantly smiled in cautious greeting. Mole returned a grimace that was revealed for what it was by the twinkle in his eye.

The others had watched this exchange with some tension which now broke sufficiently to allow Woodbine to introduce the young erstwhile gunsel to his friends.

Clae

"This be Weasel" He told them "My prentice perhaps"

The hesitant smile that Dean was sharing with Mole became genuine and unrestrained as the words crept home and nestled warm and comforting against his heart. At the sight of such obvious pleasure, Mole chuckled and Dean chuckled back until the two lads were leaning upon one another gasping for breath and wiping away tears that later would defy explanation but formed a strong bond between them that would serve them well in the future.

Little Mole joined in the mirth but his laughter gave way to a viscous cough, that left him no less breathless and teary eyed.

It became clear to Dean why Mathias had referred to baba Yaga as Mrs Catchamole. He also discovered that the mine in the hill provided coal and iron for the village, as well as other minerals that were vital to the community.

Baba Yaga was inclined to spend her time weaving cloth, her skill was legendary and her garments prized among the villagers, not least of all for the colours she could conjure from the plants and minerals about her in this strange place of rough, perhaps harsh, tranquil beauty. All three members of this group had their own reasons for shunning the society of Clae, but all three would proudly accompany the others to market day for barter and trade, each lending the courage to face those who had at one time or another judged them on their looks. They were not laughed at, or pitied, but a certain superstition that had arisen about them kept most people at their distance and of course only The Black Coven knew that they were not members of that august, arcane, disorganisation. This gave them the solitude they craved and a place in village life similar to Mathias Woodbine's position on the edges, but not out of the reach of, the community; after all they were still Clae folk.

    So there they sat, sipping a hot herbal infusion that Dean found relaxing and tasty. The mood was light as Dean had broken the barriers that held many away from this level of intimacy. As they sat and sipped a small cry sounded from a corner near the fire and it was Little Mole who rose and scooped up a child from her crib, holding her tenderly in the crook of an arm, he crooned softly to her to soothe her, as her mother and self-appointed brother looked on approvingly. Little Mole towered over Dean and offered him the chance to hold the child; Dean had no time to formulate a suitable excuse to evade the honour before he was handed the little bundle.

    He looked down into the bright blue eyes of the baby and then at the group all watching him with smiles and for reasons he could not explain, he felt like weeping.

Clae

Little Mole's huge hand fell roughly on his shoulder and rubbed his back in a friendly gesture that suggested he knew how Dean felt. Perhaps one day, when they knew each other better, Little Mole could explain it to Dean and he would know himself a little better.

Baba Yaga got up to put some more beans in the pan to feed the guests. Dean sniffed the air appreciatively anticipating the meal to come and he saw Mole nodding at him approvingly.

"It will be better for the waiting" Mole confided, picking up an axe and indicating that Dean should follow him out, the young men went to cut alder buckthorn while the older folk discussed matters that were of no concern of theirs.

Chapter Twenty Three

Dylan stretched his aching limbs as he walked slowly from the soul food cafe and back towards the generic commercial part of town with franchised fast food outlets and chain stores, in search of a haystack adrift in a world of needles.

In his search for the lost Hiawatha, he travelled to all the places he thought would attract a young lad, which were all the places he had visited when he was living here so long ago; so many experiences had trammelled his thoughts that he felt as though he had lived a lifetime in the past few days.

As he walked and searched he thought again about Clae and his vow to remain outside the Promised Land. Not that he was Moses, but perhaps he was committing a sin of pride to imagine that he could make such a negative impact on a community that had weathered the changes for thousands of years, and most of those years were spent in irregular contact with the outside world. It wasn't an isolationist policy that had kept the industrial world at bay, just a unique set of circumstances and coincidence that had preserved this idyll.

Just as it seemed that returning to Athena and Clae was the right thing to do, he remembered Hiawatha and realised he could never return unless he found the lost lad and pleaded with him to return. Then he shuddered inwardly at the prospect of Hiawatha revealing the whereabouts of the lost village and bringing the modern world crashing in on the place to subject it to forced modernisation and commodification. As he realised afresh that this would be the worst fate imaginable he realised again how he was potentially the cause of it all and once again banished himself from returning and round he went again, thoughts circling trying to catch their own tail and leaving him exhausted, dizzy and heartsick at the futility of his task.

    As his thoughts persisted in certain unwelcome directions he kept seeing Athena Slough in his peripheral vision, but turning would see just a person passing by with the vaguest most tenuous resemblance in hair colour or build. He found it exhausting to be so preoccupied and yet so concerned for Hiawatha. As he circled the market square he heard what he would have sworn was somebody calling out the name of the person he so desperately sought.

    "Hiawatha!" came the woman's voice across the lunchtime crowds, but when he looked in the direction of the call there was just a young woman running towards a uniformed policeman. Crestfallen, Dylan resumed his direction and pace looking desperately about himself in sharp birdlike movements to take in as much of the crowd as possible but feeling the futility of his search in every second that passed.

By the time the lunchtime rush had passed, and the town settled into its usual low level buzz and clatter, an inspired thought struck him and he rushed off at a tangent with a new sense of purpose.

The thought that had struck him was this; if a young man had asked a stranger where he could stay, the chances are that the person would suggest the youth hostel, or the homeless shelter. It was for this derelict, once industrial quarter of the least salubrious part of town that he now headed, with memories crowding in upon him of the tramps and drunks he had seen languishing there in the early mornings. He had a rather clear recollection of one of the old men who had a walking frame and as Dylan had passed by had awoken hacking and spluttering, with a layer of white frost on his threadbare tweed jacket. Moved by the plight of the old fellow Dylan bought him a coffee, and set it down beside the old chap, who looked askance at Dylan for one moment and then with a torrent of invective that predated the Norman invasion pitched the beverage with remarkable strength and accuracy at Dylan's retreating form. Fortunately Dylan was dressed for the cold and the liquid ran off his raincoat without causing him any physical damage, neither did he carry any psychological scars, but instead a strange respect for the fierce independence and fire in the old man's attitude to those who would patronise him.

Despite his respect, he did keep his wits finely attuned to his surroundings as he made his way downtown off-piste and amongst the scrawled railway arches and deserted warehouse buildings of the area.

The homeless shelter, with its urine musk and flaking magnolia paint, had no sign of the missing lad, and the person he spoke to there, was unable to help, as he had seen nobody of the description offered pass through the doors. Dylan suspected that the hopelessness of some of the regulars was a contagion that sapped the will to care from the person he had interrogated, until he no longer saw people and the shredded lives that brought them to the door, but merely saw empty shells that must be fed and housed and failed to notice that he was becoming as empty as they.

Dylan could think of no alternative to the shelter that would invest time, money and energy into the dignity and well being of the poor folk who arrived there daily. If only, he thought, if only he could do something really helpful for at least one of these people it would mean so much more than seeing them as a seething mass of humanities dregs, alive with neuroses, alcoholism and parasitic infestations.

Leaving the building he rested against a wall and a

woman nearby spoke to him with a thin voice but rather imperious tone,

"Would you mind awfully doing me a small favour young man?"

Dylan half expected the voice to belong to a bag lady who would probably be talking to a six foot white rabbit that only she and Elwood P. Dowd could see, but when he turned lazily and unhopefully toward her, he was pleasantly surprised to see a pair of piercing grey blue eyes focussed deliberately and intently on his face. Despite his own misgivings Dylan cautiously asked,

"What is it you would like?"

The old lady smiled, encouraged by the response, and Dylan was struck by a sense of recognition, familiarity, which he could not yet place.

"Would you sit with me and chat for a short while?"

Dylan considered his Herculean labour, his odyssey, and he sighed with the weight of it. He smiled then at the old lady and she patted the pavement beside her to indicate he should take advantage of the inviting tarmac spot being offered in order to be comfortable while she talked.

He squatted and sat heavily as he fell the last few inches to the pavement, leaned his back against the wall and smiled back at the old lady, who gathered up her hands into her lap and sent a bolt of recognition out of Dylan's blue funk and into his memory. This sweet little old lady was similar in style and demeanour to his beloved landlady, Ma Mason. Though very different in so many respects, the mannerism was so similar it caused an involuntary warm feeling toward the old lady with no home or possessions and Dylan was suddenly very curious about the path to the homeless shelter travelled by a bright eyed and cheerful old lady.

Unfortunately for Dylan, this was not a talkative old dipsomaniac who wanted to unburden herself on strangers but an intelligent woman desirous of company to invigorate her, challenge her with new ideas or to refuel her empty tank of narratives that were strange and wonderful. Her story was the tired tale that had brought her to this woeful place, so she craved the stories of others to give her vicariously, the meanings she felt she lacked.

Perhaps there is a mathematical algorithm that explains the dynamic, but when tow people who are both interested in other people get together, their efforts to tease the life story out of the other caused a positive feedback loop in which they found themselves revealing their hopes and desires to one another, both wily enough to hold back the precious, dangerous core of their being, but feeling that all else would be judged softly by the other, and like Ma Mason, Dylan had found another person with whom he would happily sit and share wisdom, nonsense or quiet as the mood would suggest.

Judith, as she quickly revealed her name to be, was interested in Dylan's family, his musical leanings and his dreams of travel. Dylan was interested in why she was here.

When he had told enough of his story to win Judith's trust, she told him hers. She explained that many women would happily marry for duty or for love, if the suitor would fit reasonably well with the expectations the woman had hidden in her bottom drawer, but if most women were honest, they settled for the man who loved them rather than holding out for the one who really matched the criteria they had mapped out at puberty and before.

Judith had married for love. A love so great that she had sacrificed the only expectation she had dared to harbour through her solitary childhood. She had been sent away to school, sent away to work, and throughout that time had imagined that one day, some day, she would raise a child to be loved by her, to be nurtured by her, to be a companion for her and she for the child. The husband had only one flaw as far as she was concerned; he had no desire for children. Judith had forsaken her dream for love, had not regretted that decision until the day, long before the dusk of their lives had started to hint at what may come, he passed away leaving her so lonely, so lost and beyond the possibility of stating a family.

The house, the home, if a house can be that without a companion to share it, all fell away to become a meaningless charade, so difficult to maintain and so easy to walk away from.

"Will you ever go back?" asked Dylan with wide eyes and more than a little empathy for her plight.

"I am resigned to solitude" Judith replied hanging her head low and shaking it in sad reflection of the events she had briefly relived in the telling of them.

"A shame you don't have some money" said Dylan, "I know somebody who takes in lodgers for company and you would be the perfect companion for her, and I think you would like her too"

"Oh I have money" Judith shot back with a little irritation at the suggestion that she was destitute. "I just have no use for it"

"Then come along and meet Ma Mason" he suggested "What harm could it do? If you don't like each other, all you have wasted is the walk, but if I'm right and you get along…"

Judith held up her chin and looked away for a few

moments as if haughtily considering something beneath her, but she soon broke the illusion with a mischievous grin and agreed to go.

"Come on then. Show me to your Ma Mason"

Holding onto Dylan's arm, they made modest progress through the streets and after the long discussion it was late by the time they were in the right part of town.

As the evening drew in the conversation had swung back to focus on Dylan again and Judith playfully pried into his fresh wound.

"What about your paramour, you sweetheart?" she enquired with a sharp elbow lightly digging his ribs. Dylan attempted to duck the question altogether.

"It's getting dark" he observed as if the obvious may be enough to put Judith off the scent, but she was the bloodhound in pursuit of his story.

"Never mind about that! What about your girlfriend?"

Dylan took a deep breath of the warm evening air and relented to reveal a little of what was on his mind.

"I have met someone" he admitted. "I don't know her very well though"

"Oh I think you do" Judith contradicted with a mischievous smile.

"No I really don't. " He insisted "We only met a short while ago"

"And yet..." said the old lady, as if narrating a scene from an theatre production "and yet... you cannot get her out of your mind. You see her everywhere and you feel comfortable by her side, and you somehow trust her to accept all that you are and feel that she could not tell you anything about herself that would make you care for her less."

Dylan had stopped in the middle of the soliloquy and was frowning at her, concerned that she had the clairvoyant gift or that he had been making his feelings and thoughts too obvious.

Judith met his eye and explained.

"You can grow to love somebody and spend years growing Marvell's vegetable love to an eventual full ripe beauty, but sometimes you can find it fully and perfectly formed. That's when it is most dangerous, because love does not exist without people: so what you develop or whatever you find, was yours all along."

"I don't follow your meaning" he said as he started walking again, but she gave no sign of having heard him as she continued.

"You see; when you meet someone and you feel love, it is your love that you feel. If they love you back it is with love they have. Loving someone doesn't make them love you and if you meet the person who brings out the love in you, it can take a minute or an hour, but if you are strong and your love is strong; whether it takes years or seconds to reveal itself, it will not easily go away again. So don't dismiss your love because it was so easily found, just be grateful you have the capacity for it and that you found someone worthy of it."

Dylan was realising that he was punching above his weight when he matched wits with this woman. He was still thinking about Athena though and spoke his next thought without meaning to.

"I'm poison to her but she doesn't know it"

"Nor would she believe it" snapped Judith. She stopped them and stepped in front of Dylan.

"I am a fair judge of character" she informed him "and I have you pretty well assessed. You do not have it in you to deliberately cause harm like that, I can see only decency and care in you, and you don't hide much"

At this point Dylan proved the point by blushing so much a streetlight that had just lit was almost shamed into switching itself off until it was dark again.

"I had such a love" she continued "I had SUCH a love. But now my love has gone and I have nothing to which I can return, my home, my heart no longer exists. I can imagine no torture that is worse than not going to where your love is. It is your love remember and if you leave it somewhere, it will die without you, and you will be forever without it and forever missing it. That part of you will be gone...forever"

Dylan met her intense gaze for a minute and began to smile.

"Husht!" she said pulling at his jacket to regain his attention "Go home if you are able. Go back to your love, or some part of you will die, and then you become somebody else."

Dylan's doubt was still on his face, so she continued.

"I gave up on a family for love. What is it you need to give up?"

"Me! Nothing! It is her...She..."

"You are smarter than I thought then, if you know what she wants and feels with such certainty that you can decide for her"

Any thought Dylan may have had of dismissing her words or ignoring her message was banished by the tears that flowed down her cheeks as she pleaded with him to follow his heart. It was the first time he had spotted the parallel stories they had told: his in its prologue, hers in the epilogue.

Clae

"Go back soon and take your chances. Let her decide" she told him

It was dark and the conversation had stalled before they were turning the corner and waddling side by side up the red brick path of Ma Mason's house and Dylan could smell the jasmine growing round the front door, excited at the prospect of seeing that welcome face once more.

It occurred to Dylan that until recently, the closest he had ever been to feeling at home was in this house, and yet he had felt at home and comfortable in Clae, more so with Athena, and now what really troubled him now that he had decided there was no place for him in Clae, was that there was no place for him outside of it either, except perhaps here at Ma Mason's house, and he was about to make that impossible too if the two women got along as he suspected they might.

Chapter Twenty Four

Hiawatha gained the relative quiet of the looped road where the traffic circled a market square which was paved over with a few ornamental trees in the centre growing where the paving was slightly uneven, unable to resist the roots as they flexed beneath the concrete, stretching languid and strong where the earthworms and soil continued the sacred dance of life where it appeared, at least on the surface, that the land had been tamed. The bulging displaced paving was just a mere suggestion of the speed at which this place would be reclaimed if people ceased to traverse it for even a short period of time. The beech trees admittedly looked like rather pathetic specimens to Hiawatha, and it was plain to see that no animals frequented them except perhaps the pigeons that seemed to have the run of the entire town centre, even in places where they could not be seen roosting it was possible to see the mark of their having been there in the acidic streaks discolouring the stonework.

He began to feel queasy, but could not identify the cause, unless it was the soft bread that seemed as though it was a stone in his stomach, or the terrible smell that was produced by the vehicles, or simply the alien environment.

The busy unfamiliar streets were not the place to escape

the claustrophobic feeling that was engulfing him like soft mud, he needed an open space where he could see more sky, and feel the grass beneath his feet; he also needed something nourishing to eat. In despair he sat on the edge of one of the public benches in the square and was immediately approached by speculative pigeons, hoping to be handed something to eat or to steal it as their courage and the opportunity coincided. Gulls were infrequent visitors to the town square but more aggressive and less bashful than their urban cousins.

Hiawatha suddenly felt very lost, and wondered if he could find his way out of the sprawling town. The town centre was positioned on the top of a hill, so as he had walked towards it this morning he had glanced back and seen the buildings stretching as far as he could see, and he wondered if Clae was in that direction or another, he was so turned about he had forgotten that he had travelled East to get here and Clae was off to the West.

As he sat and considered his next move, he was aware of a figure standing to one side of him without moving. He looked up and saw a tall uniformed man with a pointed helmet. He had heard of the Police but this was his first encounter with a representative of the legal system. Hiawatha shielded his eyes from the sun which shone behind the officer and tried to see his face, to meet his eyes.

"Are you all right son?" the police officer enquired.

"Yes, thank ye" Hiawatha replied.

The officer appraised him again to decide if the comment had been meant disrespectfully. He remained unsure so he asked,

"What's your name?"

"Hiawatha" replied Hiawatha truthfully, "Hiawatha Longfellow"

The officer was now sure that he was being ridiculed, so his next interrogative was spoken less softly.

"Where do you live?" Hiawatha blinked in silence wondering what he should do or say in this situation.

"Do you have any means of identification?" the policeman continued after an extended pause. Hiawatha shook his head sadly, as he instinctively felt that a situation was developing here that he would not enjoy, though he had no idea of what it might entail.

"Empty your pockets" ordered the policeman.

Hiawatha looked at him helplessly as he had no pockets to empty. In the silence that followed his command, the policeman looked Hiawatha up and down; at the homespun rough clothing that had first attracted his attention and saw that he had no pockets. He indicated the bag beside Hiawatha on the bench, so it was reluctantly handed over for investigation.

At that point a shrill voice could be heard across the square.

"Hiawatha!"

Both Policeman and Hiawatha looked toward the sound of the voice and saw a girl running towards them waving cardboard wrapped sandwich enthusiastically. She was still ten paces away when Hiawatha recognised her as Jenny from the Youth Club. He waved back and the policeman taking in the fact that she had called him by the name he had given and the smart attire of the young woman, suspended his investigation of the bag's contents and addressed his next questions to Jenny.

"Do you know this young man?"

"Yes" Jenny replied "That's Hiawatha" she affirmed, whilst smiling at the object of their discussion.

The policeman seemed somewhat relieved that, at least he had been truthful about his name, even it were a nickname. He pressed on with his next question.

"Do you know where Hiawatha lives?"

"He's staying with a friend of mine at the moment" Jenny replied brightly; putting out her hand to Hiawatha to clasp his own hand to imply greater familiarity than existed. Quick to pick up on the gist of her ruse, he responded in appropriate fashion.

The policeman seemed grateful that this need go no further. He handed the bag back to its owner and wished them both a good day, he walked away casually and slowly but without a backward glance.

Jenny sat down beside Hiawatha and explained her actions.

"I work over there, in the offices above the mall entrance" I was just going for lunch when I spotted you from the window and saw the police coming over to hassle you. I got over here as fast as I could to see if I could help you out."

All this time she had remained in possession of Hiawatha's hand and he was beaming his gratitude at her, but made no immediate reply. Having galloped to the rescue, Jenny considered it polite ask how he was getting along. She looked at the sandwich in her hand and considered the consequences of sharing it.

"Do you have any money?" she asked, but there was no response from Hiawatha. The aspect of his response, or lack thereof, was the fact that he had shown no hint of reaction, as if the very word was unknown to him. For reasons she couldn't explain at the time, this anti-reaction irritated her to the point of sarcasm.

"You know? Money!" she said "The stuff you buy things with. The notes and coins you need to survive. The green stuff, Dosh! The thing that makes the world go round"

Hiawatha was taken aback at the outburst but no clearer as to her meaning. For her part Jenny was immediately sorry she had responded irritably as it was crystal clear that he had meant no harm. For his part he was struggling to see how something he didn't really understand could be so vital to life. He knew about money in a vague, abstract sense but he was quite alarmed at the idea that it was a requirement for life, when he had only seen the stuff a few times and it didn't look very important, and had never been a vital part of his life. It wasn't food or drink and there was nothing else so vital, so how did these trinkets insinuate themselves onto that list?

Now that Hiawatha felt a little foolish and underinformed in the light of Jenny's outburst, so when she offered him a sandwich, his pride demanded that he refused. The doubtful expression on Jenny's face was evidence that she realised her role in the refusal. She took a small purse from her pocket and took out a five pound note and offered it to Hiawatha.

Hiawatha took it and was examining it for a clue as to its purpose, while Jenny fought a rising irritation at his behaviour, which broke in a flash of insight. She realised that his lifestyle represented a certain insecurity to her, uncertainty about where he would sleep or when he would eat, but his lack of dependence on these things and his refusal to even acknowledge the importance of money was something she envied, and not just with an abstract feeling that it could be romantic to live a vagabond's lifestyle, but an indignation that ran so much deeper, at the society that offered no choices, no alternatives that were not legally punishable or involved stepping outside of acceptable society.

Poor Hiawatha had revived her teenaged dreams of seeing more of the world, to see if there was somewhere to find the lifestyle that taunted her by hinting that it existed, but dancing out of reach in novels or anthropology articles in National Geographic, like a will o' the wisp, a phantasm for contemplating at bedtime between waking and sleep.

Neither of them was aware that the chance meeting, the exchange, the whole nexus of their encounter would not just revive those dreams in Jenny, but would awaken a passion for them, after all she had met the will o' the wisp and could no longer pretend he was imaginary, when he had looked at her through Hiawatha's eyes and taunted her with an idea; a mad dangerous idea, that suggested a way of life so different from her own that it was a little terrifying. As disturbing as it was, it began a journey that would lead her to travel to forgotten corners of the world in search of something rare and valuable; a life whose purpose wasn't abstract work, done for symbolic currency, to exchange for the highly processed necessities of life.

Jenny's search would be long but ultimately successful, though she never dreamed that the dream she pursued across continents was the reality not far from where she had grown up.

She made her peace with Hiawatha and hugged him as she left to return, distractedly, to her place of work. He turned away from the town centre and decided to get out of town. The farm had been more familiar to him than this urban maze.

The town was trickier than he thought, as he wandered along the side roads Hiawatha found roads that appeared to go where he wished ended in a cul-de-sac and he was forced to retrace his steps and try the next turning instead, only to find it looped around and took him further from his goal.

By the time the sun started to dip low in the sky, he was hungry, tired and lost; but worst of all he was still in amongst the suburbs. He decided that, on balance, it would be best to go back to the town centre and follow one of the main roads out of town.

He remembered the slip of paper in the bottom of his bag; it had an address written on it and the possibility of somewhere to stay. Plucking the slip from its hiding place he read the address with little comprehension of how to locate it. A lone pedestrian was able to direct him and he finally stood outside the house, examining its red brick path and the jasmine round the front door, comparing the number on the door to the address on the slip of paper, to assure himself that he was correct before attempting to approach.

It was a different Hiawatha that knocked on the door from the one who had left to find the world. He began to glimpse what Dylan had meant and why he had been horrified at the prospect of this kind of adventure. Individual people had been as decent as any he had known, but the faceless mass of humanity seemed to act as an enormous unthinking beast. It was that which had frightened him to the point that he knew he should return to the place where he belonged, where he understood the rules and priorities.

A middle aged woman answered the door and she gazed softly down at Hiawatha and saw the lost look and weariness in his eyes. He started to explain where he had obtained this address and why he was here, but as soon as he mentioned Sally and Joe, he was invited in and he was soon ensconced in a

Clae

soft chair with a bowl of soup, almost nodding off before his host had made a formal offer of a bed for the night.

Chapter Twenty Five

By the time Mole and Dean returned to the cabin in the rock, they had visited the nearby pond, caught a couple of fish and chopped a good quantity of nearby Alder Buckthorn ready to make charcoal. Mole had enjoyed sharing his chores and Dean had learned more about life in and around Clae. He liked what he saw and was beginning to dare hope that it would be his life too.

When the lads burst into the cabin, proud of their catch and done with the chores Little Mole, Baba Yaga and Woodbine all looked up and said nothing as if they had been discussing private matters and were being interrupted. Baba Yaga was the first to regain composure and made enthusiastic and congratulatory exclamations about the fish, taking them to the kitchen area in front of the window to clean them; one for the pot and wrapping the other in broad flat leaves for Dean to carry home to Woodbine's shelter.

Little Mole went off and inspected the charcoal fodder the lads had cut and stacked. He showed signs of approval when he returned.

"Ye did well lads" he exclaimed ruffling Mole's hair and scowling at Dean with a slight widening of his eyes and a few more wrinkles to approximate a smile as far as he was able within the limits of the inflexible leather of his features.

Baba Yaga was somehow a little too bright and cheerful, and despite Dean's pleasure in the day's activities he felt a slight chill of foreboding in the unspoken words that were held back on their arrival. However the parting was good and as Dean was about to leave with his catch when Baba Yaga stopped him with a gentle hand on his arm,

"Ye will come and see us again" she said. Dean felt it was spoken as though he was being reassured rather than invited. Little Mole patted him hard on the back and told him he would get some charcoal for his work. Mole just grinned, and now that Dean had spent time with him, grown accustomed to the way his features were uniquely arranged, he realised that whatever people may think when they met Mole, he wore a perpetual smile once you could interpret it. Never once did it occur to Dean that he had given Mole a great deal to smile about. Mole was not immune to some feelings of loneliness in the friendly isolation he enjoyed where the good folk of Clae, never went: on the occasions he went to the village, it was always with a purpose that left little time for social activities.

Mathias led the way, taking a route that passed the outskirts of the village where Dean had first arrived and then traced a path back to the shelter. Dean was beginning to build a mental map of the rough topology of this region of the environs of Clae and was now confident that he could find Woodbine's shelter again if he needed to.

When they were back at the hidden den, Dean busied himself preparing the fish while Mathias sprinkled a little of this or that herb and rubbed some fat and wild garlic into the flesh before it went over the hob in a heavy pan.

After the meal, Dean was beginning to relax again, slowly releasing the tension that had accumulated behind his concern at the truncated conversation that had troubled him so.

Mathias was darning a sock in the late afternoon sun, as Dean cleared away the cooking equipment and wooden bowls. Eventually he sat opposite the old man and admired the skill with needle and yarn. When the sock was mended, Woodbine stretched and looked about him.

"It's time" he said as if some quality of air had notified him, cues invisible to the senses of town bred folk, the likes of Dean, had prompted him to acknowledge this unchimed hour as the appropriate one for a particular action.

It was then that Mathias got to his feet and scuffled about in the sleeping area to emerge a short while later with a nylon backpack. At first Dean thought it odd that Woodbine would have a nylon backpack in such bright colours as he seemed to favour the colours of the woods, but then something tugged at Dean's memory and everything changed as the last few days unravelled and he looked fearfully at the object in the old man's hands.

Mathias said nothing, in fact he said less than nothing as he placed the backpack at Dean's feet. As Dean recognised the pack, and saw its horribly familiar logo pulling him back to recollections he would rather excise completely, a bitter bolas of dread lodged in his throat which he tried twice but ultimately failed to swallow it.

The old man revealed nothing at all as Dean looked at him for a hint or clue to the meaning of this unwelcome gift. He realised how much he had just relied upon the old fellow and now he was apparently alone in this as he attempted to extract meaning from the situation. Mathias held a closed expression on his face which conveyed only the message that the next move, whatever it may be, would be made by Dean and had nothing whatsoever to do with him.

Steeling himself against the squirming reluctance to face this at all, Dean opened the pack and gasped aloud at the shining metal of the gun as it nested among the cash he had stolen.

His heart sank and his mind raced, considering the

various possibilities this situation implied, all of which he found unpalatable, none brought him any joy.

It could be that Mathias had discovered his murky deed and was now shunning him. It could be that he was respecting their developing friendship by offering the gunsel a chance of flight with his illicit payload.

In desperate need of the old man's wisdom he looked again at Woodbine's blank face, but the old man looked away, suddenly absorbed in the careful examination of a woodlouse climbing the canvas wall.

Dean looked again at the pack, detesting it for all that it was and all that it had now come to represent, and that which he thought to escape. A wave of nausea passed over him as something of his old self lurched in the direction of self-pity, misery and, as he now realised, self-loathing.

The old man had given him a name; he had called him 'his Weasel', had suggested that he may take Baxter as an apprentice. He wondered if that exciting possibility had gone for good: if his misdeeds had found him, even here in the woods where he had started to like himself again.

Unable to explore any more possibilities without turning time and again to face himself, and the consequences of being the person he had chosen to be, something deep and visceral flipped over and latched into place.

    For the first time in his life Baxter was certain of something. He nodded grimly, closed the pack, picked it up by a strap and swung it over his right shoulder as he stood up. Without a word or a backward glance he headed for the doorway and pushed through the flap, his footfalls heavy and loud, but fading as he put distance between the old man and himself.

    The flap was caught in the breeze and not fully closing, so the daylight lit the immobile face of Mathias Woodbine, unmoving since the lad had left. The breeze fell and the flap closed and shut off the direct sunlight from the interior of the shelter but in that last flicker of shifting light, it looked as though the sunlight reflected from a single tear on the old man's cheek. In the relative darkness left behind by Baxter's departure, Mathias, once more alone, slowly closed his eyes.

    A steel resolve hardened Baxter's eyes as he trod carefully through the woodland, back the way he had come, along the narrow channel through which he had gained admittance to this sanctuary. He could have travelled more carefully as he had learned to do, but he seemed content to let the scratching stinging plants and shrubs do what they would to him as he passed. There was no regret left in his heart, no self-pity or whining complaints to be made about the unfair hand he had been dealt. This was his destiny and he was prepared to meet it in whatever form it may take.

Dylan's van marked the last point before the road and as the night drew in, Baxter trudged that long road. He didn't bother to try and catch a lift as he was walking, thinking to himself that along a country road at nightfall, it would be unlikely that anyone would think it a good idea to pick up a young, male, hitchhiker, carrying a pack. He smiled bitterly to himself as the thought crossed his mind; "After all" he thought with a bitter smile "he could be carrying a gun!"

Chapter Twenty Six

As Hiawatha struggled against fatigue in an effort to pay attention to his hosts needs, he was aware that she seemed to have a voracious appetite for information, though she was less interested in specifics, she concerned herself with the experiences that made up the life story of the person she bombarded with a barrage of friendly interrogatives. Here he wracked his brain to find a truly outstanding example of a kindness he had been shown, and before the story was full told he was being asked to recall his favourite flower, or the memory associated with a particular smell, what music he liked and what his aspirations may be.

With difficulty he managed to fire off an occasional question if he chose his moment carefully and caught her unawares, like a sniper, taking a few pot shots with queries about her own life.

From him she got a sense of a large, supportive family upbringing and a recent parting. From her he got the feeling that this was her life now, clasping little shreds of other people's stories to her to recapture something she felt she had mislaid. Hiawatha considered that perhaps that is why she takes guests, more for the company than the payment. He had been honest that he had no money when he had arrived, but had been pleasantly surprised when she had invited him in and given him soup despite his impecunious, vagrant state.

Hiawatha savoured the taste of the soup, declining the offer of bread to go with it having become wary of the deceptively soft substance that had the essence of the bread he knew but not the spirit or substance. The vengeful slices he had consumed had only just started to settle and cease to wreak havoc through his digestive tract as if resentful of being consumed. His host gathered a canvas bag as she spoke and from it she produced knitting needles and a large half complete garment in a soft wool the same shade of light brown that can be seen in dry leaves during the autumn, with a thread of a deep green in the fibre that added to the autumnal whispers of the colour.

The rhythmic ticking of the needles and the Mantel clock started to lull Hiawatha back towards dozing whenever the conversation lulled, but soon the questions would come again and the needles would tick on and the Westminster chimes of the Mantel clock would mark the quarter hour and startle Hiawatha back to wakefulness. He tried to take in the surroundings in detail, looking at the framed pictures: the walls were covered in a thick grainy paper that appeared to be made so roughly that it had wood chips visible in it. The curtains were heavy cloth but a very fine weave that impressed him, but the colour did little to brighten the room: above the fireplace hung a mirror with strange bevelled edges that made the glass appear to have a glass border without a frame. Beneath his feet was a thick carpet in the shades of early autumn leaves as they blazed orange and gold. Somehow the carpet did not do justice to these colours, appearing to be competing by making the gold too yellow and the orange too bright. It was a roll of carpet that was discovered in a shop about to close down. The price was right and the style of little consequence, so it had a chance to unfurl its thick pile several decades after its peers had been discarded, worn out, or usurped by a later style and taste.

In the wall beside the sofa was a little wooden frame with two wooden doors each was approximately square and he guessed about the length of his forearm from wrist to elbow. They were painted pale yellow, the colour of the primroses in Desdemona Pippin's garden. He wondered what these doors may conceal but checked his curiosity in favour of following the questions that still came at him irregularly. It was not until his host suggested tea that he was to find out the purpose of the doors. Tea in Clae meant a hot drink of some description, the term having long since lost its association with the exotic beverage so taken for granted elsewhere, so he had been pleased with the idea of taking tea and agreed gratefully with the offer. It was something of a shock to him when, a few minutes after she left the room, the little doors popped open as if by themselves and her voice issued from them suggesting he helped himself to milk and sugar.

    Standing up and looking through the doors, Hiawatha could see another room, obviously a kitchen. Just on the other side of the doors on a worktop, he could see two steaming cups of pale brown liquid a small jug of milk and bowl of what he assumed was sugar which was as white as chalk, not the light brown colour of beet sugar in Clae. He decided to eschew the extras and just enjoy the infusion. He first served his host with her tea, with milk and two spoonfuls of the white sugar before he sat down to taste his own cup of tea.

    It was extraordinary! A slightly bitter back taste but with some really interesting flavour which he could not describe in relation to anything else as it was so vastly different from anything in his experience. The cup itself had a strange taste rather like the soap used for washing clothes in Clae, but the tea was sublime. He was going to ask what it was but as he was about to form the question there was a sound of two bells the first high and the second low, one after the other. His host set her cup down and said,

"Oh that's the door"

Hiawatha had rapped the door with his knuckles when he had arrived so he had no clue about the doorbell. He heard a male voice in conversation with the householder and a few moments later the door closed and in walked his host with Dylan.

He stared in disbelief starting to rise but sinking back in surprise. Dylan stared back in equal incredulity the colour draining from his face as he gazed open mouthed at his Mac Guffin, Holy Grail, Rainbow's end.

It was Hiawatha who finally found his feet and threw his arms around Dylan's neck in unrestrained joy at meeting a friend, somebody who recognised him. It was while embracing Dylan that he realised how important it was to him to be where he knew his neighbours, a place where he knew who he was in relation to his peers. It was only when Dylan clapped him on the back in joy at having found him safe that Hiawatha allowed himself to feel how homesick he had become, shedding a few joyful tears at the thought that he was not alone any longer in this wider world he didn't understand, and his friend and ally was a native who could guide him quickly through this mess and back to where everything made perfect sense.

For Dylan the relief that Hiawatha was safe and well was

beyond measure. He had been charged with the impossible and had succeeded by pure chance, and could now, as long as he was willing, deliver the adventurer home again and be on his way.

Meanwhile Judith and Ma Mason had sized each other up and made tentative overtures with smiles and nods at the two lads embracing, rolling their eyes in patient amusement at the antics of youth.

By the time the adventurers had recovered from the shock of their meeting and had calmed enough to consider the situation, the two women had brewed another tea, this time in a teapot, and were sitting side by side and chattering away as if they were old friends, circling and questioning, condensing the usual introductions into a few moments and proceeding to the personal histories and deep feelings before their cups were drained and the leaves being examined with a healthy scepticism and peals of laughter.

Dylan was quizzing Hiawatha carefully about his adventures whilst careful not to reveal anything that could compromise the secret of Clae. Hiawatha was now acutely aware of the prohibition as he had gained a great deal of respect for Dylan's warnings having tasted the sour fruits of civilisation, and discovering that it was like their bread, in as much as it had the outward appearance of what it was supposed to be but had little flavour and nothing to provide real nourishment. The thought of that lifestyle infecting Clae was a nightmare so abhorrent that he felt gooseflesh on his arms at the prospect.

Assurances were exchanged quietly that Dylan was here as an expression of everybody's concern back at home, in his turn the young adventurer assured that he had come to no lasting harm and that his adventure was over without putting Clae at risk.

So absorbed were the lads in their whispered exchange that they heard nothing of the conversation being conducted by the two women until it was forced upon their notice by the gradual rise in the tempo as their chat apparently drifted downstream along the conversational continuum gathering momentum from tentative sparring to a full blooded row.

"You told him what" boomed Ma Mason "You told him that love is his! Are you mad?"

It's true though" insisted Judith "Love is not an entity that has an independent existence, it is a reflection of the capacity of two people to give love"

"But people change. What happens then?"

"Love is not love which alters when it alteration finds –

Shakespeare said that"

Ma Mason spluttered her indignation and replied

"Full of sound and fury, signifying nothing – Shakespeare said that too"

"A tale told by an idiot, is that what you're saying?"

"If the dust jacket fits..." retorted Ma Mason with a snort.

"At least I believe in love!" said Judith as if that should be the last word.

"You probably believe in the tooth fairy too" was the muttered comeback.

"Cynic!"

"Solipsist"

Dylan open mouthed in shock chose this moment to interject with alarm at the rising heat and volume of the debate.

"Ma Mason! Judith!" He exclaimed

Both women stopped and glared at the young lad. The look from Judith reminded Dylan of the headmistress at his junior school as she decided which punishment fitted his misdemeanour, now long forgotten while the feeling of intimidation lived on.

Older now and less easily daunted by authority, he met her gaze and allowed the pause to lengthen to an almost uncomfortable point before asking them both

Clae

"Is there a problem?"

The two women had until that moment, appeared transfixed by his interruption. The asking of his question seemed to dispel the tension and Judith's countenance slipped down the scale from schoolmistress to schoolgirl and she hung her head and looked a sly sideways glance at Ma Mason who was doing the same. As soon as they made eye contact, both erupted with hilarity.

"She's lovely" said Judith at the precise moment that Ma Mason declared,

"I haven't had so much fun in years"

Much giggling followed and Dylan took Hiawatha into the hallway where they could hear each other over the cackles and squawks from the two women.

In the hallway the two lads made a few brief plans. Tomorrow they should return Hiawatha to Clae and on the way they should try and find out about the River diversion to see if it was possible to do anything to help the village without exposing it.

When they returned to the sitting room, there was the syncopation of two pairs of knitting needles weaving irregular patterns about the steady metronomic heartbeat of the clock, both women smiling contentedly with no further communication forthcoming, both appeared satisfied and happy with a sparring partner and companion with spirit and wit to challenge and satisfy their individual and mutual needs.

"Love at first sight" said Dylan with a hint of irony

"Ha!" said Judith in mock contempt. Ma Mason said nothing but her shoulders shook for a moment with a ripple of ill concealed victorious mirth.

Chapter Twenty Seven

The opening pages of Fulmin Pinnock's *life of Brokken* were a repetition of the legends and stories that were well known among the village folk, although Mavis had heard none of it and although Apollo remembered far more than most, the content lacked the substance and depth they all craved. Eventually even Apollo was willing Burma to skip a few pages and find something more exciting.

Athena interrupted Burma with a suggestion,

"Why do ye not go to the last pages Burma. If The Emperor did discover something about Brokken's secret power, it would have been at the end of his investigation."

Burma looked a little relieved at the prospect of taking the short route to the information they needed, so she happily flipped to the end of the book. While she skimmed the pages for a sign that the secret was discovered and recorded here, Ballentine's librarian's instincts caused him to sift the contents of the box, among which he found a sheet which appeared to be an addition to Fulmin Pinnock's long discontinued journal.

He scanned the unsteady text with ever more incredulity:

Clae

Fulmin Pinnock XII, Emperor of Clae and Protector of the West Paddock.

I made this addition to my diary in the days after I had closed my journal for the last time, having become feeble of hand.

Spurius Lartius is a farm hand of good character, his wife is Katherine Chipping, an extraordinary seamstress with two strong sons, the first born and apprentice to Spurius is Harold Godwinson, like his father in many ways but with a deep hatred of the third war that rages about us.

Spurius informed me several weeks ago that

Clae

Harold had left the village to join the war and asked if I could help find him. It has been a while since anyone came or left the valley, so it was understandable that Spurius had some fear and concern for his son's wellbeing.

I travelled out of the village and tried my best to find him though my efforts yielded no clue or sign of Harold. It is with a heavy heart that I must say goodbye to the lad as I now know that he will probably not return, I fear he is lost to us either to the world outside or to the war.

Spurius has some comfort in the fact that his younger son, Mathias Woodbine can step in and take up the apprentice work for his father, as the Beekeeper has released him back to his family that need him.

Mathias is as wild as his brother but has a stronger sense of duty to the community, though I suspect he followed me to the village boundaries he did not, I think, follow me to the outside world. My own experience outside assures me that our isolation is now important for our lifestyle to continue; I fervently wish that no more follow Harold outside and I am now too old to make the journey again, so I allow the umbilicus to be severed and allow my trusted men to mislay the path and plant some discouraging flora along the way.

I wish Harold Godwinson the best of fortune, it is to be hoped that he is happy in whatever he has found and that Mathias can be happy without him, he was a solitary lad and perhaps had no strong bond with his older sibling to bring his sorrow.

May the world treat you well Harold Godwinson; come back to us if you may.

Fulmin Pinnock XII

The others were still straining to read over Burma's shoulder as Ballentine slipped the sheet inside a book and tucked the book under his arm nonchalantly.

At last Burma made an uncharacteristic squawk as she identified an interesting passage.

"Here it is, he says that he set a seal upon it so that it may be identified and that he would tell someone before he died"

"Tell them what?" asked Athena impatiently trying to read the page from an acute angle.

Burma flicked back a page to read the prologue to the extract she had just read.

"It says... The secret of Brokken is revealed and the treasure is a valuable one indeed as it could help Brokken stand against an army... it was... it seems it was the West Paddock."

"No!" shouted Athena with disappointed indignation which caused Ballentine to rest a finger on his pursed lips and frown at her.

Apollo asked the question that everyone was thinking.

"How did the West Paddock help Brokken fight an army?"

Burma had flipped back another page and was discovering an answer.

"There is a river underground, or a spring, which the Emperor named Brokken's River. It was held back by a dam that was starting to break down. When the Emperor discovered it and realised that it was the way for Brokken to withstand a siege, he realised he had found Brokken's secret."

A suitable chorus of "Oohs" and "Ahs" rippled through the listeners as Burma continued,

"A dam was built to keep back the Brokken River but it seems the dam may be failing again causing the West Paddock to flood; that is how he discovered the dam for himself."

"Does he tell us how to find the dam?"

Burma looked up at the others and then back to the

book, raking the page back one more leaf to reveal a sketch of the location.

"We need a few people to help" said Athena, quickly going to the heart of the matter, though she realised that it was getting late and the elders needed to be informed of what they had found and Little Mole would no doubt be needed if the answer did lie beneath the ground as the diary had implied.

Ballentine already had the tri-corn hat and hand bell, and was heading for the door with Mavis at his side.

The bell summoned the available citizens and Ballentine trusted the grapevine or bush telegraph to spread the word.

"Oh yayerz, oh yayerz" whispered Ballentine "Hear ye citizens of Clae, on this day we are saved by the warrior Brokken, founder of our village and his descendent Fulmin Pinnock, Emperor of Clae and protector of the West Paddock"

The desperate folk were stunned by the claims and were absolutely silent in their eager anticipation of some good news, and a story to go with it. This was indeed a week that would be captured in story and song for future generations to hear and remember, and to embellish with details that would elevate the yarn to a legend.

Ballentine told the story of the discovery and how it was the hope for which the village had been waiting. He also whispered that Little Mole was needed in the certain knowledge that, Little Mole would somehow receive the message but without knowing exactly how this was achieved.

The elders were informally assembled and Desdemona was looking for Athena to join them, but she was nowhere to be seen. The matriarch snagged Ben Caliban as he passed to ask if he had seen Athena but he shook his head and took the enquiry as a mandate to seek her out.

Mathias Woodbine was never seen in the heart of the village, but that didn't mean he was never there. On this occasion he was on his way back from a visit with his lady friend who lived in a croft on the far northern hillsides of Clae where her sheep grazed. The rather wonderful Virginia Creeper was about the same age as Mathias and just as weather beaten. Her solitary nature suited a lover who would visit occasionally and slip away again, leaving her to care for her sheep. Her position on the outskirts allowed Mathias to come and go with impunity and though they spent little time together they shared a fondness for one another that ran deeper than an onlooker would suspect. Virginia, like the vine, turned bright red every year, though it was exposure to the sun that from the spring was shining on her whenever it chose to shine, so her red complexion was topped up constantly through the summer months and her glory only started to fade a little as her vegetable namesake became glorious in the autumnal display.

At this point he was near enough to catch some snatches of conversation as the crowds dispersed leaving the elders still grouped in discussion.

Ballentine had reacted differently to the realisation that Athena was not to be seen; with Mavis at his side he hurried back to the sanctuary of the Manor House but too late he realised, when he got to the library the chest had disappeared.

His own secret discovery he took to the elders eventually but he was curious about what Athena may have noticed that needed to be hidden away. What was it that she could not entrust, even to him? His indignation matched only by his curiosity, but both could wait until he had a chance to discuss it with Athena.

Looking from his study window, Ballentine and Mavis saw Athena walking towards the elders to join the discussion. He shook his head and looked down as he a made a secretive smile at the thought of Athena taking the helm when Desdemona passed the duties along. He knew then that if Athena had hidden anything, it would have been for a very good reason. He also trusted Desdemona's judgement but he wondered if perhaps the unofficial apprentice was rapidly becoming more formidable than her mistress ever was, after all, who knew better than he that knowledge was indeed power.

Glancing across at the table where he had rested the book that now contained the sheet he had extracted from Fulmin Pinnock's secret cache of documents he decided that he had best give that to Athena too, after all there was nobody else of higher authority he could pass it to, now that the elders and the Black Coven had been infiltrated by her Machiavellian benevolence.

The evening light fell upon a small group gathered on the banks of the dry river Henry. The group were looking along the bank for a sign of the tunnel that should be there.

Ben moved along alone staring intently at the bank when he was startled by Athena at his elbow.

"How are ye Ben?"

"Hmph!" replied Ben a little ruffled by the surprise and still focussed on the search.

"Will ye pass along a message for me Ben?" He stopped and for the first time gave his attention to the young apprentice. He raised an eyebrow in interest and looked her in the eye, allowing her to make the request but making no commitment whatsoever to compliance.

Athena saw this small sign of indifference and realised that in order to be of any use to the community, to fill the shoes of Desdemona and Uther, she needed to command a little respect, to wield a little authority.

"The Black Coven will convene this night" she said "That is my message".

She walked away leaving Ben staring open mouthed at her. Nobody but the Black Coven had convened the Coven in his memory and now a young girl had demanded that they meet.

He considered the possible reasons why she would think she had the right, and the various possibilities of what she may have to say. Whatever she wanted them for it was probably related to the task in hand and so must be important. He also realised that she could make much mischief with the privileged information she now possessed regarding the identity of the members and the nature of the Black Coven.

Though he marvelled at her cheeky request he considered it wise to acquiesce to it, all the same.

As the searchers were increasingly hampered by the fading light they gathered again near the Manor House.

"Too dark to make a proper search now" observed Ben Caliban, looking darkly at Athena.

The others, Desdemona, Uther, Daisy Thruppence and Nebuchadnezzar all nodded in agreement. They agreed to reconvene in the morning and see if the information was correct. Athena offered to make copies of the map and instructions and the others agreed whilst little realising that Athena had her own reasons for keeping the book from the sight of other folk.

As the group dispersed to their homes, Desdemona strode away. Athena followed close behind her, glad to give Ben no chance of engaging her further. Athena was still looking over her shoulder at Uther, the master of her apprenticeship in the hope that he would not hold it against her to have gone with Desdemona. She couldn't know that Uther was as pleased with her for staying with Desdemona, as she was happy to follow the matriarch, Uther knew her health was not what it should be and Athena's regular companionship gave him some comfort.

Ben Caliban looked after Athena with a mixture of admiration and astonishment, but soon after, he went to pass word that The Black Coven would meet.

When Athena arrived home, she sat by candle light copying the map from Pinnock's book, then repeating the process. Afterwards she copied the instructions twice and only then did she sit back and wonder what had become of Dylan.

Athena was hardly aware that her training for the positions she was destined to hold in the hierarchy of the village had pushed her beyond the reach of most of the lads her own age. It was Dylan's ignorance of the situation that had allowed him to approach her on a different footing; the first person to see her as desirable, possibly attainable, a companion, an equal. In return she had impressed Dylan with her self- assurance, her warmth and her intelligence, a winning combination in anyone's estimation. She allowed herself some melancholy as she recalled his face, his smile and the music he had made to entertain them all the night before he was sent away.

Much later that night when Athena made her way to the Barrow and went in by the same route as last time, there were a few more faces there than before. She was not outwardly fazed though she appreciated the importance of this meeting.

As she climbed to her feet inside the barrow, she found herself eye to eye with a dour, leather faced man with glittering eyes and a slightly unfocussed look that disoriented her.

"Why do ye call on The Black Coven?" demanded the old fellow.

"Who are ye?" Asked Athena reasonably, as it was

unusual for people in Clae to meet somebody they did not know by name, although recently things had changed, so she was not quite as shocked as she could have been.

The stranger growled deep in his throat at her impudence before answering.

Mathias Woodbine" he told her, and despite herself Athena gasped having heard the tales, but never seen this demi-legend. She suddenly felt a few degrees warmer than before, but her die was cast and she continued into this confrontation without hesitation.

"I called ye here to tell ye something about the Black Coven" she began, but got no further as a burst of muttering drowned her speech.

When she was able to continue she said,

"Thanks to your information, I found a passage behind the wall in the library…" this time she interrupted herself with a pause because Mathias Woodbine had widened his eyes and taken a step backwards as she had said this. She correctly surmised that this was something of which Mathias knew a great deal.

"I also discovered the hidden room" She watched Mathias for further signs of recognition but there were nothing but curious wonder in his face, so she was comforted that her news may be another shock to him and the other members of The Coven.

"There were some documents in there and one of them relates to this group. It seems that in the days of Fulmin Pinnock's great grandfather, Prometheus Lucien, the founder of the Library, he needed some trusted Lieutenants to venture outside of the valley to collect his books and provide some essentials that he could not get in Clae. This work was entrusted to a group who regularly met in the barrow and quickly gained a dark reputation"

Now it was Mathias who nodded as he saw the sense in what Athena said.

"Ye mean The Black Coven was first assembled to do things for the village that the village did not know of?"

"Yes, ye have it right Mathias" she replied meeting his eye with a steady gaze.

He nodded, satisfied with the validity of the information.

"What of it?" he asked reasonably. The others were still too stunned to ask the question but now that it was out there the whole focus of the room settled again on the unimposing figure of Athena Slough. Gathering all that she had in the way of presence in the form of a deep breath and a gear change in her psyche, Athena glanced from person to person around the room.

"It may be that from time to time ye will be needed for work that aids the village but must remain secret. I hereby enlist ye for those tasks when they arise."

Incredulity created a white noise of exhaled wonder as they all exchanged glances and wondered how best to respond.

Danube Munich stepped forward with Frank Curiosity and Ben Caliban either side of him.

"What gives ye the right to..."

Mathias Woodbine held up a hand in front of Danube's face to silence him.

Mathias had seen the value of somebody who had the whole village pulse under her finger, the village square and the folk on the fringes and even The Black Coven, all understood and their needs considered. This was a matriarch to be reckoned with, the most charismatic leader the village had seen since Fulmin Pinnock or Prometheus Lucien.

Realising that she appeared to have managed her task successfully, Athena allowed herself to believe that the strength she had bluffed was hers in truth, which of course it was all along, but now that she believed it, she stood a little taller, her eyes burned with an intensity that caused Danube to shrink back behind Ben Caliban and to practically ignore Frank

Curiosity in his effort to become invisible.

"Do any of ye ever venture outside?" Athena asked.

A small gasp from several people as Mathias raised his hand tentatively.

Thank ye good people" she said. Then from inside her coat she took the book and handed it to Mathias Woodbine. "This contains some of the secrets of this group and some others besides. If The Black Coven is to trust me, then I must trust in ye all in return."

Without another word she turned her back and left the barrow as the members of the coven discussed the change in their fortunes as they had been promoted from renegade gamblers to knights in the protection of Clae.

For a moment or two, Athena rested her back against the mound outside and tried to catch the tone of the exchange, but only for a moment, before she slipped away to prepare for whatever the morning was to bring.

Chapter Twenty Eight

Dylan had insisted Hiawatha took the single bed while Dylan wrapped himself in a duvet and slept on the floor. He was too hot when he awoke but had been so tired he had slept right through despite the warm, still night. Hiawatha had still been awake processing all that he had seen and experienced, excited at the thought of returning home and pleased to see Dylan again. It was Dylan's regular breathing as much as tiredness that eventually lulled Hiawatha into a deep sleep of his own.

These factors conspired to make Hiawatha and Dylan awaken in the morning later than either had intended, sunlight bathed the room when Hiawatha opened his eyes and took stock. He looked across the room to be sure his rescuer was still at hand and there on the floor was Dylan, with his eyes open looking at the ceiling without seeing it, his thoughts far beyond the confines of the little room.

Once they were up and packed they folded the sheets and ventured downstairs to seek some breakfast. Dylan was wise to Ma Mason's food buying habits and also conscious of what would appeal to Hiawatha so he made a couple of salads from the fridge and placed one of the plates in front of his companion and saw him smile with delight and a little relief at the recognisable occupants of the plate. Mushroom, lettuce, onion, radish, tomato, rocket and beetroot were all welcome friends to Hiawatha's taste buds and even if this is not what he were accustomed to eating when he broke his fast, it was nonetheless a welcome meal.

He cut up the larger pieces of salad and wrapped them in a lettuce leaf and sat looking suspiciously at it. Dylan noticed his hesitation,

"What's wrong with your breakfast?"

"It's very cold" said Hiawatha looking carefully at the food to see if it would reveal how it could be so cold on such a warm morning.

Dylan smiled and took a knife and fork to his own plate of salad. Reassured to a degree, Hiawatha took a bite and was happy to discover that all was as it should be, though the tomato was not ripe in taste and the radish had a slightly strange soapy back taste, he ignored his misgivings and just ate.

When they had finished their food, Dylan left some money under the tea caddy and said

"Come on, let's go and say goodbye to the ladies."

In the sitting room the two adversarial friends debated anything that came to mind while crochet needles flashed in the morning sunlight and the TV news announced disasters to a heedless audience.

Judith and Ma Mason were engrossed in a debate about Christianity. Judith taking the view that the Franciscan, Fraticelli heresy was in fact the correct stance for the Church and that Christ was deliberately poor as an example to followers: Ma Mason, on the other hand, took the view that Christ was a mythological character and that his position was as an ethical blueprint and the Bible an allegory rather than a literal transcript of historical events. Such was their enjoyment of the conversation they barely noticed the two lads leaving.

Gathering up their possessions and saying farewell, the pair made their way out of the house and along the brick path to the street. Dylan took a long last look at the house and took a breath of the Jasmine scent in the air as he said a personal goodbye to this chapter of his life. Whatever came after this would be unlikely to involve returning to this town where he had been living for many months. The jasmine had been in bloom when he had first arrived and it seemed fitting that it was in bloom as he left.

Hiawatha noted Dylan's unease and asks,

"What troubles ye?"

"I thought she would be sad to see me leave"

Hiawatha considered this for a moment and then he said,

"No, ye have been spared giving her that hurt by giving her a companion instead"

Dylan smiled at the truth of the observation and slapped his friend gently on the back to get them both moving along.

Despite starting the day later than they had hoped, the shops were just opening as they got to the town centre. Dylan wanted to visit a couple of shops for some supplies. Hiawatha was intrigued as they approached the out of town shopping complex, as he had never seen such places as these.

The first port of call was a hardware store where Dylan purchased several lock knives at some considerable personal expense, telling the mildly suspicious proprietor that he was making a purchase for the local scout troop.

Next they went to the supermarket, but nothing Dylan could have said would have prepared Hiawatha for the sights and sounds that greeted him next. Firstly was a vast space, white in the light of flickering fluorescent strips that cast light in many directions and caused no shadow to be cast. He next noticed the noise, which was partly the throng of shoppers and the bleeping of till scanners, all over the background sound of a piped bespoke music station playing songs that were forty years old and between the records advertising products and services.

The rows of shelves were just a vast rack at first but as

he started to be able to adjust to the smells and noise, Hiawatha became aware of what he was seeing: row upon row of chicken, plucked and strangely shiny as though they had been stuffed in a sheep's bladder. He also noticed it was very cold near the rack and the overwhelming number of carcasses horrified him. Beyond this disturbing display was a massive collection of fruit and vegetables, some of which he recognised, such as apples which looked fresh, despite it not yet being properly the apple season. Other fruit he noticed that was also out of season but available on the shelves, including those strange curved yellow skinned delights with the soft cream coloured flesh inside.

He looked for Dylan and was suddenly horrified at the thought of being without him in this place, but he was at his friend's side smiling at his astonishment. Taking him lightly by the elbow, Dylan led the way quickly through the chaos to a rack of colourful packets, which he scanned rapidly and selected several flat blue packets of the same kind, then he scooped up several long narrow tubes from a revolving rack: he then made his way quickly to a till and picking up several packets of chocolate from the stand nearby he paid for his goods and in a few minutes they were back outside in the relative calm of the shopping precinct.

"Let's get out of here" said Dylan and Hiawatha could only look at him and nod enthusiastically to convey his appreciation of the plan.

In a few minutes they were back on the road out of town and walking to the junction where Baxter and Dylan had been diverted by the roadworks to the road which led them to Clae. A new bridge spanned the dry bed of the River which, quite a few miles downstream, had been known as the River Henry.

Hiawatha appreciated what it was they saw without explanation, and as they looked on with a form of respectful mourning for all that was implied by the dry river bed, somebody passing said,

"Oh look! That's what it will look like"

Dylan looked about to see what they had been indicating and saw an information board nearby. He went over to it with his companion eager to stay close. Together they looked at the board and saw a picture of a river going into a reservoir and then continuing to the point at which they now stood.

"Dam" said Dylan.

"What is it?" asked Hiawatha, thinking that his companion had used an expletive.

"The river was dammed" explained Dylan, "according to this information, they needed a reservoir, so they dammed the river upstream about twenty miles away, then used the time it took to fill the reservoir to make some flood defences outside of the town and to replace the bridge here making the new junction at the same time. They are nearly ready to let the river run again, later today."

Hiawatha was overjoyed at the news, and eager to get back to the world he knew, now that it would be back to normal very soon. Dylan was astonished that he had been oblivious to such a major engineering project where he was living, but he shook off his confusion to propose the quickest route back to Clae was the way he had come.

Hiawatha was amazed that just a few minutes after his proposal that they made haste, they were standing on a street corner with other people apparently doing nothing at all. It had not occurred to Dylan to explain bus stops.

The bus arrived and Dylan felt Hiawatha resist as he tried to guide him on board. Eventually they were both on board and Dylan purchased two tickets to Lower Treaton and found a seat for them both.

Hiawatha sat next to the window looking out and moaned audibly as the doors closed with a sigh of pneumatic flatulence. The bus pulled away and his fear increased with the speed. Soon they were racing along at a speed that was greater than any that Hiawatha had ever experienced and this was accentuated by the trees and lamp posts along the road that they were passing at a truly alarming rate. His knuckles white as he gripped the back of the seat in front of them, Hiawatha looked at the other passengers astonished that they sat and chatted calmly, or read books as this marvellous device roared and sped along the road. Every time it stopped and paused chugging on the roadside Hiawatha wished it was their turn to dismount, but when Dylan failed to move and the doors closed again, he held tightly onto the seat and braced himself for another terrifying ordeal.

  After a series of these terrible jaunts, Dylan stood up as the bus slowed. Hiawatha stood up too, though in his haste he was on his feet before the bus had come fully to a standstill, such was his eagerness to tread on solid ground. As the bus finally stopped he lurched into Dylan and sent them both staggering rapidly down the aisle of the bus together in a clatter of odd steps as they sought to regain their balance.

  At last they stood on the roadside, at a point where there was no bus stop and no other passengers had alighted, the driver having been receptive to Dylan's request.

  Now they set off back along the side road to the main road, so that within the hour they were looking at the sorry remains of Dylan's van and preparing for the long hike through the fringes of Clae and to Hiawatha's eagerly anticipated homecoming.

Chapter Twenty Nine

The populace of Clae were awake at first light and the crowds assembled in the village square awaiting some guidance and leadership. Uther strode into the market square with his chest out and shoulders back ready to bear that burden.

Desdemona fell into step beside him and linked her arm through his, and Uther puffed out his chest all the more and smiled at all who saw them together, as if this was the way things should always be.

Before they got to the centre of the square Desdemona eased him to a halt with a gentle pull on his arm. He stopped and turned to face her with a quizzical furrow on his brow.

Desdemona was looking at the centre of the crowd, and Uther followed her gaze and saw Athena at the epicentre, beginning to take control. Uther started to object, but Desdemona hushed him and put her arm about his waist.

"It is time we let the youngsters do some of the work" she said, squeezing him to her. Uther wasn't sure if it was time for Athena to take command, but he had dreamed of being close to Desdemona for so long he was not about to let his pride rob him of the long awaited opportunity.

Ben Caliban was given a copy of the map, Athena took another, the crowd moved off down the river bank to find the stone marker indicated in the instructions left by Fulmin Pinnock.

The crowds moved slowly along poking and scrabbling at the bank and its vegetation. Ben was shrewdly assessing the way the land was laid out and eventually decided the optimal position for the confluence and went to that spot to begin his own search. The entourage that trailed him poked about finding bits of rock and offering them to each other in the hope that they may have something of value to the hunt. Eventually a young lad named Orville Wilbur called out that he had discovered something. Ben went to the spot and tore at the weeds and grass that surrounded the spot. Sure enough he uncovered a part of a circular stone with a design upon it in a knotwork pattern and the word Brokken in the centre engraved upon the stone in a runic script.

Little Mole was suddenly there with his household, though his wife Baba Yaga and apprentice Mole hung back from the crowd. Little Mole dug around the stone and many men helped to lift it clear of the bank and rest it on the path nearby. Removal of the marker stone revealed a narrow tunnel which Little Mole was eager to explore. His apprentice bought him his lantern and some rope, but little mole was unable to get his substantial shoulders through the entrance. The apprentice,

Mole stepped up and held out his hand for the lantern at which Baba Yaga started towards him with an arm outstretched in protest, but she was too late as Mole took up the rope and slipped inside the hole with the lantern held in front of him.

Athena was there by this time, and the crowd allowed her to get close to Little Mole and Baba Yaga who waited by the entrance. All were silent in anticipation of some signal or sign from Mole inside the tunnel. After a few minutes of shuffling noises, a muffled voice could be heard.

"It opens up some, after a little way, gaffer"

"Go steady young 'un" called back Little Mole, holding the end of the rope that Mole laid as he went, "We will dig out around the entrance some"

Carefully to prevent any collapse, Little Mole began to clear the excess around the hole, removing some stone pieces of some considerable size so that the bank was similar to a stone wall with a wet clay mortar. It seemed to take an awfully long time to make progress and before they had made much headway, Mole popped his head out of the hole and announced he had run out of rope.

Little mole looked across the paddock to the tree line of the woods and the foot of the rocky hill and calculated the length and direction of the tunnel from the rope already laid down along it and shook his head.

"Mole is already at the foot of the hill, we need to open up the mouth of this tunnel before he goes back down its throat"

The workers all took a bite of lunch and some water as volunteers cleared more of the wall which remained stable with no collapse of walls or roof so that Little Mole allowed Mole to convince him that he should go back down with some extra rope. If the instructions were correct he should soon get to the dam and tie his rope to the brace.

Athena asked for horses to be brought to pull the brace when it was found and runners were despatched to fetch them. A few people were stationed at intervals to pass a signal along the river bank to Shylock Giza at the mill so that he could react when and if the water was restored. He didn't want a flood at the millpond or to have the wheel damaged by a torrent.

Taking a deep breath as if ducking under water, Mole prepared to go back into the tunnel. Little Mole stopped him with a restraining hand and shared a look which they both understood. It was a long practiced exchange between men in a dangerous profession that said I make you this promise, that I shall watch your back; try to keep you safe if the effort should kill me; it was all the insurance they had. Baba Yaga stood silently to one side having managed, over time, to approximate a fortitude that she didn't actually possess, for she feared for her men whenever they went into the Earth.

Mole took the extra rope and started down the tunnel. He had learned over time to feel as well as see his way about. Knowing what the route feels like is as important as being able to see it as the light is a luxury that cannot be guaranteed. The floor and walls were wetter and muddier as he wriggled along until he found the end of the rope he had left along the route. Taking the rope he had about him and unfastening the end, he quickly tied the two ends together. Feeding out the rope as he went, he struggled along down the sticky muddy channel.

Holding up the lantern provided no sign of the end of the tunnel but he still had plenty of rope to feed out though he hoped that he would not have to go back again for another coil of rope, unsure if his courage would be ready for a third test of its strength. Again he held up the lantern and there at the limit of his light was a thick wooden structure across the width of the tunnel. One solid brace came from the centre and was buried in the floor of the tunnel.

Mole knew better than to rush. Even with his objective in sight he made cautious progress. At last he was within reach of the brace and he rapidly fed out the remaining rope and tied the end securely to the base of the bracing timber, appreciating that it was a solid timber which was in fact just a small tree trunk that had been roughly hewn for the purpose. He was partially immersed in mud and water at this point, the River being held back was escaping through and around the blockage as well as it was able.

With the rope secured and only the lantern to carry back he turned around to head back. The movement brought him into contact with the tunnel roof and part of it fell with a soggy plop, causing Mole to freeze and assess the movement before attempting to continue.

As he waited, he decided all was stable and he started to move towards the exit. He had moved about the length of his own body when the walls flopped in upon him and for a moment he was submerged in water and mud. As he spluttered and lifted himself up to keep his head near the roof of the tunnel and to breathe, he realised that the water had doused his lantern.

He resigned himself to a dark journey back. In the blackness it was easy to imagine the pinprick of light in the distance that meant safety was nearby. Now the rope was secured to the brace it could not be used to pull him to safety if he should be buried in mud. He pushed those thoughts aside and moving more swiftly he crawled in darkness back along the tunnel.

The afternoon was dragging along and the horses cropped the edges of William Absurd's fields as the village folk waited with some anxiety at the mouth of the tunnel, while Little Mole continued to direct a few to move the stone and clay that supported the walls and narrowed the entrance.

The steady constant pace that Little Mole maintained was more to allay his concerns that any need to push himself so hard. He was so intent on his task that he didn't notice much else until Athena shouted out beside him.

"Water! Look water"

It had suddenly occurred to her that the muddy bed of the Henry was wetter than when they had arrived and now there was a small rivulet running along the bed, but not from the tunnel, not the River Brokken they were trying to free; this was from the source of the River Henry and it was gaining strength as they watched. Athena quickly commanded everyone to get out of the river bed, and in a few moments all but she and Little Mole had complied. Little Mole was still wearing his usual expression but his voice shook as he leaned into the mouth of the tunnel and said

"I don't see his light"

Then he bellowed down the aperture

"Mole! Mole! Get ye out of there"

As he stood up Mole's head popped out of the entrance and he looked a little pained as he looked at Little Mole.

"Awright Gaffer, ye near popped my ears"

Little Mole plucked his apprentice from the hole and pushed him up the bank and then turned and did the same with Athena before scrabbling up there himself.

The crowd watched fascinated as the rivulet became a trickle and the trickle seemed to be steady at that and no more, so they turned their attention back to the rope extending from the mouth of the tunnel.

Fastened to the harnesses of the two horses on the opposite bank they started to walk along the bank downstream as the tunnel formed a "Y" shape with the river bed, the slack rope was soon taken up and the horses leaned into the load and strained.

All the while Mole was drying in the sun, mud caked on every inch of clothing and exposed skin. He was the centre of much admiring attention and a couple of young girl's hearts were beating a little faster at the thought of being there when the hero had saved Clae. They all had a sense that history was being written today and they all felt a part of it. To the people who owed him a debt, Mole was less strange looking and more of a daring adventurer at that moment. It was doubtful that he would ever find himself feeling like an outsider in the village ever again.

He was cheered and slapped on the back as the hero of the hour, the one who was about to save Clae, standing a little taller than before and appearing a little less odd than before.

Nothing happened with the horses still pulling against the load. They sweated and strained but no sign came from the tunnel at first. Then there was a loud rumble from the tunnel and at the same moment the horses surged forward and the assembled crowd felt a trembling under their feet as the River Brokken came tumbling along its tunnel removing the loose soil and bringing down parts of the walls and roof of the tunnel as it went.

Then it came; dirty, sludgy brown, it surged from the tunnel and kept on pouring out bringing forth great gobbets of clay and mud, pieces of the restraint that had held it back for so long, stone from the narrow entrance as it was washed away until the Henry started to look more like its old self.

Shylock was notified by a series of signallers to prepare for the water, so he opened the channel and allowed the new flow to bypass the millpond and flow away into the underground course of the Henry in the Western hills.

Uther and Desdemona restrained the young people from jumping into the water in delight, but encouraged the jubilation of the folk as they capered and shouted in delight at the sight of the life returning to the village.

As the river Brokken flowed strong if not yet clear, the crowd noticed the river Henry was starting to gain strength to the point that where the tunnel had been was fast becoming the confluence of the two.

A celebration was beginning to develop as the heroes and the rivers were exalted, Mustik was fetched and beer was given out to all. Shylock Giza returned from the mill and joined in the merriment. Nobody but Desdemona noticed that Athena was not present. As soon as Athena saw that the village was now saved, she realised that her life of duty to the village was important but she also felt lonely and torn by her feelings for Dylan. The happy crowd were too much for her now that the task was completed and she fell back to the thoughts that she had pushed aside for this purpose.

Desdemona found her at the brewery and already knew what was wrong.

"Ye spend your whole life working for them"

"I do" said Desdemona softly putting her arm about the

shoulders of her young apprentice.

"Is it worth all your effort?"

Desdemona chuckled heartily,

"What a question" she says "Well, the only other option is to serve only yourself; now that never gave anybody any joy. If you look after the village, the village will reward you in ways you can't even imagine and would think me a liar if I told you. But you will find out in time"

Athena rested her head against Desdemona and sighed.

"I know ye are missing him. If he doesn't come back I'll have to say I was wrong about him. I'll tell ye this too, if he does stay away; every time he thinks of ye he will strike himself for a fool.

"Come now child, the village is wanting to thank ye. Don't stay away when times are good"

Reluctantly, and with her heart elsewhere, Athena allowed herself to be led back to the joyful reunion of Clae and the River Henry.

Chapter Thirty

The route into Clae seemed to be worse than before. Dylan followed Hiawatha and seemed to snag his bag or his clothing on every branch and thorn along the way. Though it weighed him down and dragged against him he did not give it up, pulling it to himself with one hand and scrabbling at the banks and hillside with the other.

Several times he had to request that Hiawatha allow him to rest for a short while. His mind was racing as he considered options and possibilities.

He wondered if his influence would be as damaging as he suspected, but considered that a child learns to grow protective and slightly suspicious of others in the world in which he grew up, so even someone as resolutely optimistic about human nature as he tried to be, would eventually adopt an attitude that in Clae would be considered cynical; that factor alone made him the serpent in Eden and barred him from returning. But then there was Athena, the most remarkable woman he had ever met: Her open hearted, acceptance of him had humbled him and made him feel unworthy of her; how on Earth could he pass up the chance of building something of a life with her?

Then again, if his toxicity was as highly contagious as he

feared, would he ultimately bring misery to her too, and if so, how could he live with that?

Round and round he went, with nowhere near sufficient attention to his travelling as was required to stop him being torn and scratched as he passed along the route.

Eventually, he became aware of Hiawatha becoming eager to press ahead so he called a halt.

"You go on ahead. I'll catch you up later" he said, though his inability or unwillingness to make eye contact was communicating a vastly different message.

Hiawatha stopped and struggled with his own conflicting urges, one to bring his friend along to Clae and the other to rush home as swiftly as the path allowed. He looked properly at Dylan for the first time since they had set out on the wooded path and saw he was striped with grazes and quite tired, his clothes torn and grubby. He felt guilty for setting a punishing pace for poor Dylan who was obviously struggling to keep up.

"I shall walk slowly from now on" but Dylan just smiled and shook his head.

"No! You go on. I shall be fine"

It was then that Hiawatha realised that Dylan was not going to go with him back to Clae. He couldn't understand why and under the circumstances he was far too willing to accept the decision at face value and be on his way home. It was conscience that held him back, to understand what it was that stopped Dylan returning with him.

"You are not coming back, are you?" he asked bluntly.

"Yes I am. I just need to rest for a while" Dylan replied without trying to invest the statement with any conviction. Hiawatha may have been naive, but he could recognise an outright lie.

"Please! I can wait for ye" he begged. Dylan just waved at him to go.

"I'll be along later" he repeated.

Hiawatha looked along the path and back at Dylan, he had no idea of what response to make to this persistent lie. His home was horribly close and he wanted no more delays, not even for this important issue. It was seemingly intractable and the effort seemed wasted, so he took solace in the fact that he had tried but had ultimately left Dylan to be the master of his own destiny.

He embraced Dylan briefly and looked at him one last time to fix his face in his memory, then he turned and continued on his way, at a slower pace despite his enthusiasm for a homecoming, just to allow for Dylan to have a change of heart within the next few hundred yards.

Nobody followed him, and the single glance over his shoulder that he allowed himself, revealed that his view had already been obstructed by the undergrowth.

Ahead he thought he could hear laughter on the breeze. He pushed his way onward and through the last bushes on the edge of the paddock and saw jubilant villagers laughing and dancing, entertaining one another with poetry and song, while Burma was telling a suitably adapted version of the recent events to her group of young learners, who sat wide eyed and attentive as she embroidered the events with little artistic thrills which are second nature to storytellers.

He was part of the way across the Paddock when somebody shouted and he was soon mobbed by the good folk of Clae, pummelling him with questions, news, welcomes, hugs and kisses.

As the chaos gradually subsided and he had gasped the briefest account of his adventure, he was allowed some refreshment and a short respite. Once rested it was expected that a full account of his adventure be related to the assembled crowd.

As he rested and took some food and drink, Athena made her way to him and stood before him saying nothing. Hiawatha suddenly found the food difficult to swallow and needed a considerable draught of cool water before he could attempt to speak.

"He didn't come back with me" was all Hiawatha could say without repeating the lie that Dylan had told him.

"Will he come back?" asked Athena at last, though she feared the answer, she was one for facing things directly and she had to know. Hiawatha's answer was to look away at the hills he had just crossed, but being unable to meet her steady gaze until he heard her sob.

Athena refused to lose control in front of the crowd, but Desdemona was nearby and aware of the implications of Hiawatha returning alone, swiftly led Athena away from the group, across the paddock toward the hills from which Hiawatha had emerged a short time ago.

She realised that attempting to follow him was pointless. If he didn't want to come back to her, he wouldn't want her to go to him. She had to face the fact that he did not want to be with her. With only Desdemona to see her so vulnerable she leaned into the older woman and wept as Desdemona smoothed her hair, and clucked sympathetically like the mother hen she was born to be.

Dylan watched as Hiawatha took a half dozen steps

before disappearing from view. He considered how out of place he felt in the world, but here, in this place, this idyll, he felt as though he represented the big bad world outside, soiling the paradise with his bitter experiences of a less trusting life.

He moved to turn away from paradise, uncomfortable with his reserved place in Eden. For all of his dreaming, he now wondered if he should deny himself entry to the Promised Land for fear of destroying it with his mere presence.

As he turned away his bag snagged on a branch and he realised he had forgotten that he had the gifts still in his bag. A moment of hesitation gripped him as he considered returning to distribute the gifts but realising that it would be for his own benefit alone, and could do more harm than good, he turned again to retrace his path back to the wicked world outside.

One step was all he managed before the ground gave way beneath his feet and he was dunked in water. When he surfaced spluttering and coughing he realised it was quite dark and there appeared to be nowhere to get out.

Grabbing at the muddy wall to check his progress further downstream where the flow was attempting to drag him, he looked upstream and saw the place where he had fallen. It appeared he had fallen through the roof of a tunnel that a river ran through. He doubted that it was the River Henry as that was further to the East but at this moment survival was more important that knowing which watercourse was attempting to finish him.

Clawing at the muddy clay of the walls and bobbing down to the bed and up again to the surface he struggled back to the gash of light where he had found his way in. The side was a gentler slope where he had caused subsidence of the edge, but he was still too wet and slippery to gain purchase on the sides. He tried to push up and grasp the bushes he could see peeking over the ridge of the slope, but he fell short and grasped a fistful of mud which came away in his hand. Another try and another fistful of mud and he realised that he was tiring quickly and may not have been able to manage another attempt. In his panic he found an adrenal burst gave him the push he needed for another attempt at the ridge but as his hand grasped mud another hand grabbed his, and pulled against the drag of the water.

Dylan got his feet on the bank and climbed as fast as he was able while the hand pulled on his arm and between them walked him up the bank and onto dry land. For a few moments both men caught their breath and Dylan was at last able to seek the identity of his rescuer, who met his gaze with a small smile.

Dean Baxter was not as muddy as Dylan, but a fair few thick splashes now decorated his clothes. The smile made Dylan realise that this was not the desperado who had kidnapped him, but a new, improved version of the one he had met. What else could he do but return the smile?

"That wouldn't have happened if you had been going the right way" Baxter observed.

"I was just leaving" Dylan joked without much feeling.

"Why?" asked Baxter, genuinely puzzled by the thought.

"There's no place for me here" Dylan replied without being quite sure why he should be telling this to Baxter of all people. After all it should be Baxter who stayed away, being representative of a far more corrupting influence than Dylan ever was.

"That's a lot of crap" Baxter opined without invitation.

"Listen" he explained "If Clae has a place for the likes of me, it has a place for you too." He paused to consider some private thoughts and then added "It is perfect."

"Where are you going anyway?" asked Dylan.

"I'm going home to Clae. I had some stuff that wasn't

mine and I had to return it."

They exchanged a glance that made them both smile.

"Well thanks for saving my life" said Dylan as he started to get to his feet and check the contents of his bag and see that everything was still there.

"You're not still leaving are you?" asked Dean.

Dylan nodded sadly.

"You don't want to leave do you?" asked Dean.

Dylan shook his head slowly with equal solemnity.

"Seriously" said Dean, "If you don't belong here, you're never gonna find a place to settle. This is it mate, this is the place."

Dean saw with uncharacteristic perception that he was having an effect.

"Do I have to force you there at gunpoint?" he asked with a smile.

"Not this time" Dylan replied.

The two walked side by side to the edge of the scrub and rock where the River Brokken now cut across the paddock and Dylan saw where he had been taking his involuntary dip earlier.

Dean stopped before he was out in the open.

"This is as far as I go" he explained. "There is a place

for me here, but not in the village"

"You saved me twice now" Dylan told him "I won't forget it" Dylan extended his hand as a gesture. Dean eyed it for a moment before taking the hand and shaking it.

"If you ever need me, come and find me" said Dylan as he released the handshake.

"I think we are even now" came the reply "but I will come and see you sometimes, if you don't mind"

"You will be welcome" Dylan assured him. Dean's response was to offer his hand again, though this handshake was more genuine and firmer than before though just as brief. Dylan also took one of the lock knives from his bag and offered it to Dean, who took it with an enthusiastic grin. This was worth more to him than words.

Without any further exchange Dean turned on his heel and walked back into the thicket and as he disappeared from Dylan's view he came face to face with Mathias Woodbine looking at him in such a way that Dean felt the need to explain himself.

"I put it right" he told him.

"That ye did" replied the old man looking at Dylan as he walks away. "Well Weasel. Are ye ready to be my prentice?"

"Yes Gaffer, I am" replied Dean Baxter, one of three new

residents of Clae.

"Good lad. Now get back and make some supper while I go and take care of some business"

Pleased and honoured by the assignment, Dean went off to do what he was asked.

As Dylan emerged from the trees and it was Athena that spotted him first. She could not at first believe what her eyes were telling her, but Desdemona Pippin confirmed her sighting.

"There's your fine lad" she told Athena, "Now go and get him"

Athena, waving her arms above her head in greeting started to walk towards him as the gathered mass of folk realised what was happening and began to move towards Dylan as a single entity.

Before they get there a lone figure emerged from the scrub land and intercepted him by stepping in front of him. The whole crowd halted in awe as the Beekeeper rarely emerged in public events and if he had something to say it was an occasion that would go down in history, such was the reputation of his monumental reticence.

Athena stood at the front of the surging crowd and Dylan stood facing them, between these two factions stood the

Beekeeper facing Dylan, appraising him, to make sure that what he had thought of the lad on their first meeting was still true.

Nobody spoke as the tension mounted, intimidated and awed by the aura of gritty silence that surrounded him, unlike the delicate hush surrounding Ballentine; this was a more dour abhorrence of speech that meant that few had heard him speak.

Nothing was said as the two men looked at each other for a long few moments, and then the Beekeeper surprised everyone by stepping close to Dylan and ruffling his hair. "Welcome home lad" he said before walking back into the woods approving of the fact that Dylan made no reply.

Everybody was slightly shocked and impressed with Dylan, wondering how he managed to make an impression and win the respect of the Beekeeper after so short a time.

With Dylan now free to be assaulted with a thick battery of questions and welcomes, he was at a loss until through the crowd Athena managed to find her way to him and stood before him looking for the first time in her adult life like a small child, almost bashful. Dylan tried but could not say a word, as he knew not how to begin to explain his confusion and apparent contradictory behaviour.

Again the crowd had fallen silent as they felt the gravity

of what was passing between them, as Athena looked sideways at Dylan with her arms hanging limply at her sides she rested her weight on one leg and asked softly,

"Where are ye going?"

"Wherever you go" he replied. Somebody in the watching group said "Ahhh!" and Athena stepped close to Dylan and pressed herself against him and her thin lips against his: Dylan felt he had returned home as he appreciated more fully the profundity of the words he had spoken.

Despite his muddy clothing and the damp mud still clinging to his bag, he rummaged in it and produced the packs of needles, giving one to Desdemona who glanced suspiciously at the pack and then her eyes widened as she realised what it was and she looked at Dylan in a way that made him appreciate the local value of the gift.

Dylan still held several packs and Desdemona eyed them with a shrewd glance.

"Did ye bring those to trade?" she asked indicating the packets in his hand with a nod of her head.

Dylan glanced at the packs as he tried to work out what she may be implying.

"I think Baba Yaga would make good use of a pack of those" she said. Everybody murmured agreement, after all, that household had earned the respect and admiration of them all that day. Cautiously Mole stepped forward to accept the gift that Dylan now extended towards Desdemona, and as the two met face to face, both covered in the wet muddy clay of the Brokken River Dylan just smiled and put the pack into Mole's hand. Their eyes met and both nodded a quiet understanding that had been reached in those few seconds. Mole knew that here was someone else with whom he may share some company in time.

Baba Yaga did not step forward but she did accept the needles from Mole as he found her in the group and the small group quietly disappeared before any realised they had gone.

The end is nigh

Along the Treaton Lane before it joined the main road into town was a gravel lay-by where the Farmer turns his tractor without having to hold up traffic on the main road, but on this occasion it has been borrowed by a small convoy of military vehicles, pulled over and stopped as if it were a very small car park.

The uniformed driver stepped smartly out of the centre vehicle and stiff backed, he opened the passenger door. He stood to attention as a grizzled officer of extremely high rank climbed out of the vehicle. Almost immediately there were two security officers at his elbow, scanning the horizon for any threat.

"Stay here while I look around a little. I was stationed here once. Nostalgia and all that"

"Sir...?" began one of the security men, but he was waived silent by the officer.

"I am aware of the dangers and I won't be going too far. Stay here!"

He walked the few yards to the junction and crossed the road to disappear into the tree line on the far side of the road. The security detail exchanged looks but remained where they were, as they were accustomed to some odd behaviour from officers and this was not a person to question.

A few yards into the woodland and the officer encountered a rusting van, crunched and lifeless, with the faded legend of Lucky Sid's legendary business on the side panels. From the woods emerged Mathias Woodbine who stopped and looked at the officer with some shock apparent on his face, though he wasn't caught unawares by the stranger.

"Mathias"

"Harold" replied Woodbine.

"The Henry is flowing again then?" said Harold, as a statement of fact, rather than the question it may have appeared to an onlooker had there been one.

"Yes" replied Mathias "Back to strength." He took a bottle from his bag and handed it to Harold, who held it with something like reverence.

Is this"…?" began Harold

"Mustik" said Mathias helpfully finishing the sentence that had faded away.

"Last year's Mustik" he qualified.

Harold's eyes sparkled as he looked at the bottle.

"Was it a good year?" he asked, but Mathias shook his head in response.

"I don't drink it anymore" he admitted, and the

incredulous look Harold shot at him was soon replaced by one of impressed surprise when the steady gaze with which Mathias met his, was one of serious resolve. He could only nod his respect for the choice and say no more. Another awkward pause fell between them.

"Will you ever come home?" asked Mathias eventually.

"One day, perhaps" replied Harold. Their eyes met once again and both men stepped forward and embraced.

When they stepped apart again, Mathias turned without a word and started back into the woodland, but Harold called after him.

"Be careful Mathias, these woods are Ministry Of Defence land and have been the site of a small accident involving a radioactive agent."

Mathias turned back to Harold and stared at him for a long moment.

"I saw the signs and the fencing going up. What do you know about it?"

"I filed the report myself Mathias. This place is not safe to visit for at least one thousand years due to the nature of the experimental device and the unexploded ordnance around the ranges"

Mathias nodded, and smiled at this.

"Thank ye, Harold. Ye are still the older brother, still looking after me."

"Goodbye Mathias. Be safe"

Both men turned and left, to return to the life that each had chosen; Mathias Woodbine to watching over Clae from a distance, and Harold Brown to his own life in the military where he too managed to watch over Clae from an even greater distance.

The security officers said nothing at all about the bottle of clear liquid that he cradled as he got back into the car, assuming that there was something afoot that was beyond their security clearance, which in some ways, there was. Harold Brown was looking forward to a nostalgic taste of his youth later that evening, and to remember the unofficial secret he had kept for all those years since he had been Harold Godwinson.

Chapter Thirty One

The sun reluctantly set on the lively festivities that took place in Clae's heart, while the folk who live in and around the village realised that the crisis had passed and life could return to its usual leisurely pace.

Shylock Giza held the attention of the youngest villagers with a puppet show that illustrated the importance of home and community, while Hiawatha watched from the sidelines basking in some attention yet nodding wisely at the emphasis of the drama. It featured a wandering rabbit sent scurrying home by the attentions of a hungry fox.

Ballentine had been encouraged by Mavis and her enthusiasm for the celebration, to remain out of doors longer than was his custom. He didn't appear to resent the disruption of his routine, in fact he was grinning with pride as one or another of the villagers made a point of becoming acquainted with her.

Daisy Thruppence was eager to meet the newcomer, greeting Mavis with her typical emotional effusion. Her tough brown hands were gripping her shawl at the neck when it caught Mavis' attention.

"What a beautiful shawl!" she exclaimed "Did you make it yourself?"

"Goodness! No. This is one of the beautiful cloths Baba Yaga makes."

Mavis was peering with critical appreciation at the fine weave and the stitching, reliving her happiest memories of making and adjusting clothes for people in the days when it was sensible to mend clothing, to patch trousers and to darn socks. The satisfaction and the use of her skills had been something she had really enjoyed, but had only just realised it.

Looking around her at the people she could see, there were patches and repairs, hand-me-downs and adapted items everywhere. Ballentine took notice as he saw his Mavis come to life again with even more passion than he had suspected she could contain. He recognised the signs having seen apprentices matched with their skills over the years. He knew that the shawl had revived in her something bigger than the deep affection they shared, something more powerful than the home she had found. The elusive, slippery, intangible and life affirming prize that Mavis had found, was a purpose.

Ballentine's intense interest in this was partly his generous nature taking vicarious pleasure in her discovery and partly the selfish knowledge that a purpose was the key to happiness and longevity, both of which were to his distinct advantage.

Daisy and Mavis discussed plans and ideas, exchanged tips and gradually attracted a group of individuals who shared their interests.

Elsewhere, Uther had initially been a little put out that Athena had been given the authority to lead the village through the recent crisis, but as he was now able to enjoy the undivided attention of Desdemona Pippin he had begun to perceive the advantages of allowing a new generation to shoulder some of the burdens of leadership and allow the older folk to indulge their own hobbies and passions.

The Black Coven having discovered an exciting new aspect of their organisation, were positively itching to meet and uncover the secrets in the book they now held. They were among the first of the throng to depart and apparently head for home. Eventually they would head out to their dread meeting place where the cribbage board would gather dust for a while as they explored the origins of their secret society.

Danube Munich, the youngest of the Black Coven members was sent to speak with Apollo Brokken, the resident expert on the ancient history of the village and a favourite to join the Coven and bring his perspective to the texts compiled by the illustrious Fulmin Pinnock XII.

Athena and Dylan were left alone to get reacquainted on the banks of the River Henry which flowed high and clear past the distillery and off to the mill. Dylan recalled the contents of his bag and pulled out the slender tubes that had puzzled Hiawatha when he had purchased them.

Each tube contained a pair of magnifying spectacles of

varied strength, not prescription but sufficient to allow the older citizens to see more clearly when they were sewing, reading, writing or carving by candlelight. He gave them to Athena in the certain knowledge that their distribution would be handled well. Beneath the glasses cases at the bottom of his bag Dylan discovered the chocolate he had bought.

Little Mole, at the head of his table, expressed some small regret that he would not get to hear Dylan play the guitar music that he had heard about. Baba Yaga looked up sharply with a note of yearning in her eyes at the mention of music. Mole too looked a little pained at the prospect of missing the entertainment.

As Baba Yaga solemnly placed a Beech bowl of stew in front of each person at the table it was Dean who introduced a note of optimism.

"I think he may come here and play for you"

Mole, who had shared a moment of understanding with Dylan, was alone in daring to believe that it could happen.

"Why would he?" asked Little Mole doubtfully.

"Perhaps he owes Weasel a small favour" Said Mathias with a wink at Dean. Baba Yaga was smiling again as they broke the thick loaf and began to eat.

Clae

Dylan and Athena sat on the banks of the River Henry as he gave Athena a bar of chocolate and she examined the mud splattered wrapping wondering what it was, so he unwrapped the bar and offered her a piece of the confection. Athena cautiously took a small bite and closed her eyes to focus her senses on the texture and taste of the chocolate. Dylan lay back on the grass and waited while considering that it was a link with the world outside and he considered that world in all its strangeness with some good and some bad.

Athena had now experienced the chocolate melting and has tasted it properly and is quite surprised by its peculiar properties.

"It is almost too sweet and then it is bitter too. I don't think I like it very much"

Dylan was still thinking about the world outside Clae, but he found that he had to agree.

Epilogue

So as the sun sets on Clae at the end of another day, the naming of that day can be allowed some regional variation, but the same sun sets on the village as beyond. The same sun will rise in the morning and life goes on.

Of course, you superior specimens of humanity, fulfilled in your lives with every electronic convenience and food from across the globe available in a cellophane package in any season from the supermarket, will doubtless close the book and give silent thanks that you do not have to endure the lifestyle these unfortunates must. Let this be a cautionary tale then, so you not forget that your participation is required to keep alive the fast paced, convenience of modern life, then go and precipitate it lest we fall into the trap of building communities, having real conversations with real people, caring about them and having them care about us in return. Such primitive lifestyles are not for the sophisticated denizens of the 21st century, so close the book and think no more about Clae, or somewhere like it that exists just out of reach in the soul of every human being.

Clae

Printed in Poland
by Amazon Fulfillment
Poland Sp. z o.o., Wrocław